Secret Admirer

Other books in the growing Faithgirlz!™ series:

Bibles

The Faithgirlz! Bible
NIV Faithgirlz! Backpack Bible

Bible Studies

Secret Power of Love
Secret Power of Joy
Secret Power of Goodness
Secret Power of Grace

Nonfiction

My Faithgirlz Journal
The Faithgirlz! Handbook
The Faithgirlz! Cookbook
No Boys Allowed
What's A Girl To Do?
Girlz Rock
Chick Chat
Real Girls of the Bible
Faithgirlz! Whatever
My Beautiful Daughter
Beauty Lab
Body Talk
Everybody Tells Me to Be Myself, But I Don't Know Who I Am
Girl Politics

Fiction

From Sadie's Sketchbook

Shades of Truth (Book One)
Flickering Hope (Book Two)
Waves of Light (Book Three)
Brilliant Hues (Book Four)

Boarding School Mysteries

Vanished (Book One)
Betrayed (Book Two)
Burned (Book Three)
Poisoned (Book Four)

Sophie's World

Sophie's World
Sophie's Secret
Sophie Under Pressure
Sophie Steps Up
Sophie's First Dance
Sophie's Stormy Summer
Sophie's Friendship Fiasco
Sophie and the New Girl
Sophie Flakes Out
Sophie Loves Jimmy
Sophie's Drama
Sophie Gets Real

The Girls of Harbor View

Girl Power (Book One)
Take Charge (Book Two)
Raising Faith (Book Three)
Secret Admirer (Book Four)

The Lucy Series

Lucy Doesn't Wear Pink (Book One)
Lucy Out of Bounds (Book Two)
Lucy's Perfect Summer (Book Three)
Lucy Finds Her Way (Book Four)

Check out www.faithgirlz.com

faiThGirLz!™

Secret Admirer

GIRLS OF HARBOR VIEW

Melody Carlson

ZONDERVAN.com/
AUTHORTRACKER
follow your favorite authors

ZONDERKIDZ

Requests for information should be addressed to:
Zondervan, 5300 *Patterson Ave. SE, Grand Rapids, Michigan 49530*

ISBN: 978-0-310-73048-4

Art direction and design: Cindy Davis
Interior composition: Ben Fetterley

Printed in the United States of America

12 13 14 15 16 17 18 19 20 /DCI/ 17 16 15 14 13 12 11 10 9 8 7 6 5 4 3 2 1

So we fix our eyes not on what is seen, but on what is unseen, since what is seen is temporary, but what is unseen is eternal.

— 2 Corinthians 4:18

Ski Trip

chapter one

"This has been the best Christmas of my entire life!" Carlie said happily as she helped her mom clean the kitchen. It was the day after Christmas, and according to Mom their house was "a big fat mess." Although Carlie didn't think it looked that bad. Still, she hadn't complained about helping this morning. Mostly she just wanted to get these boring chores finished so she could get to the clubhouse in time for this afternoon's meeting.

Her mother stopped scrubbing the countertop and peered curiously at her now. "What made this Christmas so special for you, Carlotta?"

Carlie paused from sweeping as she considered an answer to Mom's question. The truth was Carlie wasn't *only* thinking of Christmas with her family, although it had been nice enough. The truth was she was thinking about her friends too. She was thinking of the fun she'd had with them, and better yet the fun that was just around the corner. But if she said that it might hurt Mom's feelings. So she just shrugged. "I don't know ..."

"It was a nice Christmas ..." Mom continued scrubbing

out the sink. "But we did the same things as always. Tia Maria made her same Christmas empanadas, we sang the same songs, you and your brothers and cousins did the same Posadas … and Pedro put the baby Jesus in the same manger and we had a piñata … all just the same as always. So tell me, mija, what made this Christmas your favorite?"

"I just mean that *everything* has been so great this year, Mom, and Christmas with the family was really good. But I was also thinking how this is our first Christmas living here in Boscoe Bay, and how it's my first Christmas in junior high. And how it's been fun doing things with my friends, like being in the Christmas parade and our Christmas party in the clubhouse …"

"Oh." Mom nodded as if taking this in.

"But Christmas with family was great too," Carlie said quickly.

"And I suppose you're looking forward to the big snow trip with your friends?"

"Well, yeah …" Carlie smiled sheepishly. Okay, so Mom had hit the nail right on the head. "That's going to be pretty cool too."

Now Mom's brow creased with worry. "Oh, mija, you must promise to be very careful up there. Tia Maria reminded me that she sprained her ankle on a ski trip in high school. We don't want you getting hurt or breaking anything."

"Don't worry, Mama. I'll be careful."

Mom nodded, but still didn't look too convinced. "And your friend Emily ... does she get to go on the snow trip too?"

"Yes, Mama." Carlie carefully swept the small pile of dirt into the dustpan. She knew her parents had been pretty upset over the recent situation with Emily and her family. They hadn't said much to Carlie, but she'd overheard them discussing concerns about Emily's dad and whether or not the neighborhood was safe with a man like that in town. Although, Carlie was fairly certain he was still safely locked up in jail after breaking and entering when he was trying to force his family to leave with him. Even so, Carlie had heard her father say that he was going to be on a special lookout ... just in case the creep showed up again. For that matter, the whole neighborhood would be watching for him. Carlie thought that was probably a good thing. No one wanted anything bad to happen to Emily or her family.

"And Emily's mother isn't ... well, she's not worried at all?"

"I think her mom is just thankful that they got back home in time for Christmas," Carlie said carefully. She knew that it was always best not to worry her mother. For some reason Mom worried a lot. She worried about other people's problems and worried about her house not being clean enough. Carlie mostly didn't get it. But that was her mom.

Just then Carlie heard her little brother Pedro screaming like he'd been hurt — probably pushed down by four-year-old Michael again.

"There they go again," said Mom.

"I can finish up in here," Carlie said quickly. "If you want to go check on the boys."

"Thanks, mija," Her mom peeled off the rubber gloves and handed them to Carlie. "What would I do without my girl?"

Carlie didn't answer that one, but she had a pretty good idea of what her mom would do without her. She'd probably pull out her hair and scream so loudly that Mr. Greeley would come running with his shotgun. Carlie knew that Pedro and Michael pushed Mom's patience to the max, but being the older sister of those wild little boys was no picnic for Carlie either. And even though Mom paid her for babysitting — *sometimes* anyway — Carlie could hardly wait to escape her rowdy brothers for three precious days.

She sighed as she washed the stovetop. In her mind's eye she could see the pristine mountain, not so different from the photo on the brochure that Morgan had first shown them. And Carlie could imagine the white snow and the peaceful calm of being outside. Better yet would be hanging with her friends. But the best part of all would be not having to wipe a runny nose or scrub a sticky face or tell a screaming boy to "just be quiet!" It would be so awesome to be at the ski lodge, hanging with her best friends and no little brothers. It sounded like heaven to her!

In fact, that's what today's meeting was about. The girls were gathering at the clubhouse to try on ski clothes and pack and plan for the trip. Fortunately, Chelsea had lots of snow clothing to share with the others. She had wanted them to come up to her big fancy house to try things on, but Morgan had talked her into coming to the clubhouse instead. And Carlie had been glad to hear that. In Carlie's mind, the clubhouse was their own special place ... and just because Chelsea didn't live in Harbor View shouldn't give her the right to try to change things. Sometimes Carlie felt like the original four girls — Morgan, Emily, Amy, and her — had to stand their ground with Chelsea. But she knew that wasn't a very good attitude. And really, most of the time she liked Chelsea.

As Carlie cleaned, she planned what she might take on the ski trip. Unfortunately, she didn't have much in the way of ski clothes, although her aunt and uncle had gotten her a pale blue belted parka for Christmas. She couldn't wait to show it to her friends. Really, this had been an awesome Christmas break so far. And it was only going to get better.

As she scrubbed the bathtub, tossing her brothers' tubby toys into the mesh bag, she mentally checked off what she might pack for the ski trip. Nothing fancy, of course, just some sweatshirts and her favorite jeans and maybe her Tommy Hilfiger warm-ups. Carlie frowned as she remembered how she'd been influenced by Chelsea last fall, being talked into spending way too much money for certain items of clothing. Carlie wasn't into that anymore. Wasting money on designer labels just seemed plain stupid now. Of course, she wouldn't say that to Chelsea.

Finally, it was nearly two, and Carlie was done with the bathroom that she shared with her brothers. Sure, it might not be as perfect as Mom would like — since Mom was, after all, the Queen of Clean — but it was close. And, at least it smelled good now. That was challenge enough with her two little brothers and their messy habits. As she went out into the hallway, she noticed that the house had gotten nice and quiet, and Carlie suspected her brothers were already down for their naps. She went to her room and threw some things in her duffle bag to take to the clubhouse. It seemed sort of dumb now, but Chelsea had insisted that they all bring what they intended to take on the ski trip. She said this was going to be a packing party. The best part was that Chelsea was bringing "refreshments."

"Running away from home?" asked Mom when Carlie nearly ran into her in the hallway.

"No." Carlie grinned sheepishly. "It's our packing party. Remember, I told you about —"

"Yes, I remember." Mom nodded. "Just teasing."

"Well, it is kind of silly ... but Chelsea is the fashion expert, you know, and she wants us to look our best."

"Nothing wrong with that," said Mom. "I always want my family to look nice." She ran her hand over Carlie's shoulder-length dark curls. "And I like my girl to brush her hair and —"

"I know, Mama." Carlie glanced at the clock. "But I'm already running late."

"Okay ... have fun."

Carlie quietly closed the door behind her and slung the strap of her duffle bag over her shoulder. It felt so good to be outside. Even with the damp chill and the brisk breeze, Carlie would much rather be out here than in a stuffy house. She breathed deeply, letting the sea-scented air fill her lungs, and holding it a long time before exhaling. Some people, like Mom, didn't like the smell of the ocean. Mom often said that it smelled dirty — like rotten fish and old seaweed, but Carlie thought it smelled full of life. In fact, Carlie sometimes thought she might like to be a marine biologist. Either that or she'd like to be a landscape designer, or maybe work in forestry. Whatever Carlie did, she knew it would be an outside job — and she would never have to comb her hair if she didn't want to, and she could get her hands just as dirty as she pleased.

"Hey, Carlie," called Amy Ngo as she jogged up to catch her. Like Carlie, she was lugging a bag too. "You're late."

"Just a few minutes," said Carlie. "But I'm surprised *you're* late." She grinned down at her petite friend. "Little Miss *I Hate to Be Late.*"

"Yes, well, I had to work lunch at the restaurant today. My sister An took off without telling anyone."

"Where'd she go?" Carlie was curious. Of all of Amy's older siblings, Carlie liked An the best.

"No one knows," said Amy mysteriously. "She disappeared last night after work and never came home."

Carlie blinked. "Are your parents freaking?"

"A little. But, as you know, An is an adult — she's twenty-seven. I guess if she wants to take off, she should be able to."

"But what if something's wrong?

Amy giggled. "Well, Ly is saying that An probably eloped with her new boyfriend."

"Eloped?"

Amy nodded with a sly grin. "But I don't think so."

"And you're not worried?"

"An has a good head on her shoulders."

"Yes," agreed Carlie. "But I hope she's okay."

"She's just teaching Ly a lesson," said Amy as they reached the clubhouse, which they'd converted from an old hippie bus. "They got into a big fight at the restaurant yesterday."

"Well," said Carlie as she opened the door. "That explains everything."

"Hey, it's about time," called out Chelsea as the two of them entered the bus. Carlie was glad to see that the others were already there. She took in another deep breath as she closed the door behind her. Like the sea air, Carlie liked the smell of their old clubhouse too. Oh, she was sure that her mother would not approve. She would probably think it smelled musty and in need of a good cleaning, but Carlie always thought the clubhouse smelled more like an adventure about to begin. And usually that was the case.

chapter two

"You girls ready for the fashion show?" asked Chelsea as Carlie and Amy sat down on the couch.

"Fashion show?" Carlie frowned. What was Chelsea up to now?

"We're going to take turns going down the runway," explained Chelsea. "Morgan and I will take turns designing outfits, and everyone will take turns modeling them."

"You're not serious?" Carlie glanced over to where Emily and Morgan were sitting at the little dining table, and they just nodded.

"It's Chelsea's idea," said Emily.

"But it'll be fun," said Morgan.

"Toss your clothes into the bedroom," commanded Chelsea. "We're going to do a little mix and match."

"I think it sounds great," said Amy with excitement. "Who gets to go first?"

"How about you?" suggested Chelsea. "And I brought some ski clothes that I outgrew — they might be perfect for you."

And so Chelsea and Amy went back to the bedroom,

and Carlie tried to convince herself that this wasn't ridiculous. Oh, Carlie was well aware that Chelsea was big into fashion. Of course, Chelsea had the money for it. But then, to be fair, Morgan was into fashion too. But Morgan always took the creative approach.

"Cheer up," said Morgan. "This is going to be interesting."

"Start the music," called Chelsea. "Model number one is ready for the runway."

Emily jumped up and went to the old-fashioned record player and turned it on, and suddenly Amy emerged. She was dressed in a puffy pink jacket, black pants, and a hot pink polar fleece hat that Morgan must've made. Her outfit was completed by an oversized pair of dark glasses with rhinestones around the edges. Looking like a petite model, Amy came strutting down the makeshift runway (the center aisle of the bus) and did a nearly perfect turn, except that she bumped the record player and made the song skip.

"Oops." She put her hand over her mouth.

"Amy, you look fantastic," exclaimed Emily.

"Yeah," agreed Carlie. "And that jacket looks like it fits."

"It's a little big," Amy admitted, allowing the sleeves to slip down a little. "But a pair of gloves might help keep them up."

"Good job on model number one, Chelsea," called Morgan.

"Emily is next," yelled Chelsea from the back. "I've got some things all ready for her."

So while Amy strutted back and forth a couple more times, with Morgan doing an off-the-cuff commentary on the stylish snow outfit, Chelsea helped Emily get ready for the next portion of bus fashion day.

As it turned out, the fashion show was fun. And Carlie was pleasantly surprised when Morgan put together a pretty cool outfit for her. Carlie never would've thought to pair a leopard-print scarf with her pale blue coat, but it actually did look good.

"We are going to be styling up on the mountain," declared Chelsea when they were finally finished.

All the girls had packed their bags for the trip now and were kicking back and enjoying a junk-food fest (compliments of Chelsea).

"Now if we can just snowboard as good as we look," teased Carlie.

"I'm going to ski," said Amy.

"Not me," said Morgan.

"Or me," said Emily. "We're riders."

Amy frowned. "Isn't anyone going to ski?"

"I don't know," admitted Carlie. "I've never done either."

"Well, I'll bet the boys will all be snowboarding," said Chelsea.

"Like we care," said Carlie.

"Hey, some of us might care," said Chelsea.

"That's right," added Amy.

Morgan, Emily, and Carlie exchanged glances, and then Morgan just rolled her eyes. "To each her own, I guess."

Carlie shook her head. What was wrong with Chelsea and Amy? Why this sudden interest in boys? "So, is that why you're so into clothes?" Carlie asked Chelsea. "Because you think the boys will care?"

Chelsea just shrugged, but Carlie suspected she was right.

Morgan laughed. "Boys don't seem to care about their own clothes, why should they care about ours?"

"Oh, *they do*," said Chelsea, nodding like she knew. "Trust me, they really do."

"How do you know?" demanded Emily.

Chelsea just laughed. "If you have to ask, you wouldn't understand, Emily."

"That's right," said Amy, suddenly acting like she was so grown up and not really the youngest of the five girls. "If you have to ask, you really don't get it."

"You mean you get it?" persisted Emily.

Now Amy laughed. "Duh."

Emily turned and frowned at Morgan and Carlie.

"I think these girls are jerking our chains," said Morgan.

"No way," said Amy. "Think about it. All of my siblings are in their twenties ... you think I don't know a thing or two about guys and romance and things like that?"

"I think this conversation is stupid," said Emily. Then she got up and went to the record player, flipping over the album and turning up the volume. "And I think we should dance!"

Soon they were all dancing, and all the silly disagreements over boys, and whatever, vanished into the thump-thumping sound of the bass. And that was how Carlie liked it to be. Just girls being girls and having fun. She didn't see why Chelsea and Amy wanted to change things by dragging talk about boys into their clubhouse.

Finally it was getting late, and the girls knew it was time to pack it up and head for home. "Tomorrow's the big day," Morgan reminded them. "Does anyone need a ride to the church?" As it turned out, they all did. Well, everyone but Chelsea. That was no surprise. Chelsea's mom always seemed to have time to chauffeur her around.

"My grandma still isn't supposed to drive," Morgan told them. "But my mom said she can come home from —"

"My mom can take us," offered Chelsea. "No problem."

So it was settled. They would meet at Morgan's house

at nine and ride to the church with Chelsea. As they left the clubhouse, Carlie noticed that Amy was sticking to Chelsea like superglue as they led the way back to the mobile-home park. She even invited Chelsea to wait for her mom to pick her up at her house. And, for a change, Chelsea agreed and didn't even seem to mind hanging with Amy — probably because of that stupid thing about boys.

As usual, Emily and Morgan were paired off, walking up ahead of Carlie on the sandy trail. Suddenly Carlie felt totally left out. In the past, she was usually stuck with Amy. Okay, "stuck with" wasn't a nice way of putting it. But sometimes Amy and her perfectionist ways got on Carlie's nerves. And sometimes Amy even reminded Carlie of her mom. Even so, it was better than being left out ... better than being alone.

"See ya in the morning," yelled Morgan as she and Emily headed over to her house.

"Be there or be square," yelled back Amy as she and Chelsea went across the street to her house.

"Bye ..." called Carlie, feeling lame and left out as she trudged back to her house.

"Hey, mija," said Mom as Carlie came in through the kitchen door. "How was your meeting?"

"Okay ..."

Mom leaned down and looked into Carlie's eyes. "Something wrong?"

"No," said Carlie in a sharp tone.

"Well." Mom stood up and blinked.

"Sorry," mumbled Carlie. "I better go finish packing my stuff."

"I have a surprise for you."

Carlie looked at her mom with interest. "What?"

"You go finish packing, and I'll get it."

So Carlie went to her room where she began stuffing things like socks and underwear and T-shirts into her bag.

"Is that how you pack?" said Mom as she came into her room with something behind her back.

Carlie looked up and frowned. "Yeah."

"No, no, no," said Mom as she sat down on the bed, setting down whatever it was she had behind her. Then she removed several items of wadded up clothes from Carlie's duffle bag, carefully laying each item out on the bed and smoothing it, then she folded them — perfectly. "Like this," she told Carlie. "Then you won't be all wrinkled when you get there, mija."

"I don't care about wrinkles," grumbled Carlie.

"But don't you want to look nice?"

Carlie shrugged. "It's a ski trip, Mom. Who cares how you look?" Of course, even as she said this, she knew that her friends — at least some of them — cared.

Then Mom reached behind her back. "I got you something for your trip," she said as she produced a pink and white polka dot bag.

"What's that?"

"It's for your personal items, Carlotta. You know, things like toothpaste and deodorant and even lip gloss." She smiled as she held up a cherry-flavored stick. "And I filled it up for you." Then she held the bag out to show the contents.

"Uh, thanks." Carlie forced a smile.

"And I want you to use these things, mija. You don't want to go around like a bum for three days, do you?"

"No..."

Mom frowned now. "I thought you had started to care about your appearance, mija — when you and Chelsea went shopping for school things."

Carlie nodded. "Yeah, I do care." Mostly Carlie had been relieved to be freed from wearing all the frilly, little-girl clothes that her mother had been so in love with. And she'd been thrilled to cut her long curls. But, most of all, Carlie just wanted to make her own decisions when it came to her appearance. She didn't want her mom telling her how to do her hair or folding her clothes or picking out lip gloss for her. Really, was that too much to ask?

Mom patted her head now. "You're such a pretty girl, Carlotta. I just always want you to look your best."

"I know..."

"And you're getting to the age when you'll start to care

more too. And . . ." Mom giggled. "You'll realize that boys are starting to look your way and — "

Just then both of Carlie's brothers started wailing and crying like someone was being murdered. For once in her life, Carlie was glad to hear them getting into a great big fight, probably over a new Christmas toy or the remote control to the TV. But they were really getting into it.

"You finish packing." Mom quickly stood. "While I go break it up."

Then after Mom was safely out of the room, Carlie quietly closed her door, muffling the sounds of her screaming brothers. Once again she began wadding up her clothes and stuffing them into her duffle. She didn't care if they were wrinkled. Weren't they her clothes? Didn't a girl have the right to wear wrinkled clothes if she wanted to?

After she was done making a fine mess of her bag, she picked up the frilly looking pink and white polka dot bag and just stared at it. It looked like something Amy would like, but it definitely was not Carlie's style. What was Mom trying to say to her anyway? That Carlie needed to look or act like Chelsea or Amy? Did Mom want Carlie to act silly and get boy crazy too? Even so, Carlie felt a little guilty when she shoved it into the top drawer of her dresser and slammed it shut. There — that was just where she intended to leave it!

Carlie wasn't sure why she felt so strongly about these

things, but she did. She wanted to be her own person. She didn't need Mom or anyone else telling her how to act and dress! She could take care of herself!

chapter three

As Carlie carried her duffle bag over to Morgan's house, trudging down the street in the chilly gray morning, she felt uneasy. Maybe going on this ski trip wasn't such a great idea after all. What if Morgan and Emily paired off ... and what if Amy and Chelsea paired off ... and what if Carlie was left on her own? What would she do? Still, she had worked hard and paid a lot of money for this trip. She couldn't back down now. Besides, all four girls were her friends. They wouldn't just abandon her — would they?

Later on that morning, as all five girls filled up the two backseats of one of the church vans, Carlie couldn't help but feel better. Here she was with her four best friends, laughing and joking and going away for three whole days of fun and snow. With no little brothers to take care of, and — even better — no mom to tell her how to dress or act.

"Woo-hoo!" yelled Carlie as they pulled out of the church parking lot. Her friends all echoed her woo-hoo with gusto, and then they all burst out laughing. Carlie grinned happily as she sat in the backseat with Morgan and Emily. Life was good!

"I'm so glad you got your beads back," Carlie told Morgan as she gave a couple of the beaded braids a friendly jingle. "I didn't want to say anything, but I thought your beads were so much better than the curly look."

"Me too," admitted Morgan.

Carlie tugged on one of her own curls. "Sometimes I wish I could do something like that myself. Then I wouldn't have to brush my hair every day."

"Why don't you?" asked Morgan.

"No way would Mom let me. She thinks it's bad enough that I cut my hair. If she couldn't see my curls, she'd have a fit."

Chelsea turned around in the seat in front of them. "I wonder how I'd look with beaded braids," she asked as she patted her red curls.

Morgan seemed to study her seriously, but it also looked like she wanted to laugh. "It might work."

"I'm so glad the boys and girls are riding in separate vans," said Emily.

"Not me," said Chelsea. "I think the boys kinda spice things up."

"You mean stink things up," said Carlie. She stuck her nose in the air as if to make her point, and they all laughed.

"Hey, did you guys meet Whitney yet?" asked Morgan quietly.

"I did," said Emily. "She seemed nice."

Amy turned around now. "Who is she anyway?"

"She's the girl with short brown hair sitting next to Janna in front," said Morgan.

"Who's Janna?" asked Chelsea.

"She's the youth leader," said Emily with an impatient tone, like she wondered if Chelsea ever paid attention. "The one who was standing with Cory when we prayed in the parking lot."

"She's really pretty," said Chelsea.

"Anyway, Whitney is Janna's youngest sister," continued Morgan. "Janna's parents just moved to Boscoe Bay a couple weeks ago. Whitney will be going to school with us after the new year."

"Yeah," added Emily. "And Janna asked us to make her feel at home."

"Are we there yet?" whined Chelsea, and everyone laughed since they were barely out of town.

"I'm hungry," teased Carlie. That was one of Pedro's favorite lines.

"I need to go potty," added Emily.

Janna glanced in the rear view mirror. *"You guys!"* But then she was laughing with them. And before long, she had them all singing those corny kinds of camp songs that everyone says they hate, but somehow everyone knows the words to and enjoys singing them loudly. Naturally, Carlie was no exception. Good thing she'd gone to day camp a few times before they'd moved to the coast. And she had to admit, at least to herself, she kind of liked the funny old songs. Plus, they helped pass the time.

About two-thirds of the way there, they stopped for an early lunch break, pouring into McDonald's and confusing the cashiers as they made, then changed their orders. Finally it was sorted out who got what, and Cory told everyone that they had just fifteen minutes to chow down if they wanted to get any skiing in today. Of course, that got everyone moving quickly, and before long they loaded back into the vans. They arrived at the ski resort just a little past noon, and everyone piled out of the van and immediately started throwing snowballs and jumping into the mounds of snow heaped alongside the parking lot.

"Let's unload our stuff," Cory yelled at the kids. "And dump it in our cabins so we can hit the slopes ASAP. You guys only have a half-day lift ticket for today, but you better get moving if you want to use it."

Everyone scrambled to get their stuff piled onto some of the sturdy-looking luggage carts that a couple of the boys had rounded up.

"Okay, girls, come with me," called Janna as she pointed down a trail. "Our cabin should be right this way."

"Hi ho, hi ho, it's off to the snow we go," sang out Morgan, and soon the others were singing with her, making up more new and even sillier words as they marched along.

"Here we are," announced Janna. She opened the door to a high-ceiling cabin filled with six sets of bunk beds. "It's not the Ritz, I know, but I think it'll do for the next couple of nights." Then she opened a big yellow envelope and handed out ski passes as well as cafeteria passes. "The cafeteria passes are just for lunches," she explained. "We'll all be eating together in the Spruce dining room for breakfasts and dinners. But lunch is sort of a free-for-all." Then she gave them each a schedule as well as a list of rules. "I don't want to have to say too much about the rules," she told them. "I'd like to think that you girls are mature and responsible. We tried to keep the rules simple ... mostly common sense and a few manners. We do want you to have fun, but we want you to be considerate of others. We're not the only ones using the slopes."

"So, Janna," said Morgan, sounding slightly impatient, "When do we actually hit the slopes?"

Carlie tossed her backpack onto a lower bunk, and then Emily snagged the bunk above it. But, like Morgan, Carlie was feeling impatiently eager too. She couldn't wait to strap on a snowboard.

"Okay, I'll try to keep this short," said Janna. "But before you all take off, I want to introduce everyone to everyone. We left town so quickly that we totally forgot to do that." She had the eleven girls stand in a circle then said a quick prayer, asking God to keep them all safe and to make these three days very special and memorable. After that, she asked the girls to go around the circle and tell everyone their name, age, and favorite food. "And you better pay close attention," she warned them, "we'll have a few more *favorite* questions in the next few days, and whichever girl remembers the most facts could win a pretty nice prize by the time we leave."

Naturally this got their enthusiasm going, and Carlie decided she would pay careful attention — the idea of winning a prize was appealing.

"Since I haven't met everyone yet, I'll begin," said Janna. "Obviously, I'm Janna Olson. I'm married to Cory, the youth pastor. I'm twenty-five, and my favorite food is pasta — *any* kind of pasta." She patted her waist, which was actually fairly slender. "If pasta didn't have so many carbs, I'd probably eat it three times a day." They all laughed, and then Janna pointed at her younger sister. "You take it away, sis."

"I'm Whitney Phelps, I'm thirteen, and my favorite food is sushi."

"Cool," said Chelsea, who was standing next to her. "Sushi is my favorite too. I'm Chelsea Landers, and I'm also thirteen." She jabbed Emily who was standing beside her. "Next."

"I'm Emily, uh, Chambers — "

"Huh?" said Janna with a confused expression. "I thought you were Emily Adams."

"My real name is Chambers," said Emily. She looked embarrassed, and Carlie felt bad for her. "It's a long story, but my family and I will be going by Chambers from now on."

"Oh." Janna nodded slowly. "Okay, continue."

Emily smiled at everyone. "I'm also thirteen, and my favorite food is pizza with lots of cheese."

"I'm Laura Miller," said a plump girl with frizzy blonde hair. Carlie had noticed her in school before, but had never really spoken to her. "I'm fourteen, and my favorite food is french fries, although my mom keeps telling me that carrot sticks would be a better choice."

Chelsea snickered, and Carlie wanted to punch her.

"Next," said Janna, nodding to the tall, thin girl with long black braids and a not-so-good complexion. Carlie already knew her name was Julie because she'd gone out for soccer, although she wasn't very good. But that was about all she knew about her.

"I'm Julie Bryn, I'm fourteen too, and my favorite food is the same as Janna's. Pasta."

"What's up with you skinny chicks liking pasta?" teased Laura.

"I'm Cassie Caldwell," said a short girl with long

brown hair. "I'll be thirteen next week, and my favorite food is peanut butter and banana sandwiches."

"Just like Elvis Presley?" said Morgan.

Cassie nodded. "Uh-huh. My grandpa is a huge Elvis fan, and he told me about the sandwich."

Now it was Carlie's turn, and she made a face, hating to admit her age since everyone usually thought she was older. "I'm Carlie Garcia. And I'm still just twelve, but not for too much longer. My favorite food is my mom's apple spice empanadas."

"Mmm," said Janna. "That sounds good."

"I'm Morgan Evans, I'm thirteen, and my favorite food is pizza." Emily reached over and gave her a high five.

"I'm Amy Ngo and, like Carlie, I'm twelve, and my favorite food is chicken quesadillas."

They continued around the circle with Erin Simpson and Taylor Richey, two fourteen-year-old eighth grade girls who Carlie had seen around school, but didn't really know. Apparently they were best friends and had been in youth group longer than anyone, and they both liked vegetarian lasagna.

"Well, all this food talk is making me hungry," said Janna. "And I'm sure some of you are itching to get on the mountain. But before we go to the rental place, for those of you who need equipment, I want to point out the first rule on your list. The buddy system." Janna looked out over the group. "The thing is, skiing and riding can be dangerous, and we do not want anyone out there on their own. So we're all pairing off right now. You will be responsible for your buddy, and your buddy will be responsible for you. You'll probably want to choose a buddy whose skiing or riding ability is at about the same level as yours. If you decide to switch buddies, you have to make sure that everyone's in agreement and that I am aware of it. Does that seem reasonable enough?"

They all immediately agreed, and suddenly everyone was deciding whom to pair off with, and Carlie wasn't sure what to do. Chelsea grabbed Emily by the arm. "Come on, Em," Chelsea said eagerly. "Let's be buddies. You're a good rider, and so am I."

"I, uh, thought I'd be Morgan's buddy," said Emily, looking at Morgan hopefully.

Morgan nodded and stepped next to Emily. "Yeah. Sorry, Chelsea. Emily's been my teacher; I need to stick with her."

Chelsea frowned then turned to Carlie, like she was a second choice, but might do in a squeeze. Naturally, Carlie found this slightly irritating. "Are you going to snowboard, Carlie?" Chelsea asked.

She folded her arms across her front now, unsure as to whether she wanted to be paired with Chelsea or not. Yet at the same time, she didn't want to be left out. "Yes," she admitted, "I thought I would try it."

"So you've never ridden before?" asked Whitney with interest.

Carlie felt self-conscious now. "No, not really …"

"How about skateboarding?" asked Emily. "Have you ever skateboarded?"

Carlie brightened. "Yeah. My best friend before we moved here was a skater, and her big brother made a half-pipe in their backyard. I used to borrow a board and do that with them sometimes."

"Were you any good?" asked Whitney.

Carlie shrugged. "I guess I was okay."

"Well, that's a lot like snowboarding," said Emily. "You'll probably be fine. I've been teaching Morgan to ride on my skateboard, and I think she's going to be okay too."

"So want to be my buddy, Carlie?" asked Whitney.

Carlie was surprised and relieved at the same time. Still, she wasn't so sure she wanted to be stuck with a girl she didn't know. But she didn't particularly want to be stuck with Chelsea either. Mostly she didn't want to be left by herself. She smiled at Whitney. "Sure, why not?"

"What about me?" asked Amy. "Who's going to be my buddy?"

"But aren't you skiing?" asked Chelsea.

"Well … I was … but maybe I'll snowboard instead." Amy smiled at Chelsea in a hopeful way. "Do you want to be my buddy, Chels?"

"But you don't even know how to ride, Amy."

Amy looked hurt now. "I can learn."

"Maybe I should ride with Amy," offered Carlie. "The beginners could stick together."

"No," said Whitney stubbornly. "You said you'd be my partner."

"But maybe Chelsea would be better for you," suggested Carlie. She grinned now. "Besides, you both like sushi."

"You were paying attention to that?" said Chelsea with surprise.

"Sort of …"

"Maybe we can all sort of stick together," offered Emily. "I mean, since we're all snowboarding. We can see how it goes, and if some of us are better riders than others, we can switch buddies." She glanced over to where Janna was pulling on her ski clothes. "Is that okay, Janna?"

"Sure," called Janna. "Just as long as no one gets left on their own. Whatever you do, let's get going. We're burning daylight, girls."

chapter four

Suddenly the room got very noisy as the girls started opening bags and layering on snow clothes. Everyone was excited and happy, and Carlie couldn't wait to try out a snowboard. She just hoped she wouldn't slow down Whitney too much. It had been sweet of this new girl to be willing to risk it with her. Carlie wasn't even sure why she was being so nice, but she suspected it wouldn't be too long before Whitney regretted her choice. Maybe she would discover that Chelsea was a lot better and want to switch buddies. Then Carlie would be stuck with Amy. It's not that she didn't like Amy, but Amy just wasn't very athletic. Carlie would be surprised if she was coordinated on a snowboard. Still, it would be better than being alone.

"Okay," called Janna. "The girls who are renting equipment, come with me."

It took about an hour to get the right boots and boards, and by the time Carlie and Whitney were finally riding up the bunny-hill chair, it was past two. "This is going to be a pretty short day," said Whitney.

"That's okay," said Carlie happily. "We still have two more."

Then, as they rode up, Whitney gave Carlie some pointers on how to ride, talking about balance and how to lean and how to use your hands.

"Do you think I should go to the beginners snowboard class tomorrow morning?" asked Carlie. Suddenly she felt uncertain. What if this was really hard?

"Let's see how you do today," said Whitney. "You might not even need it. I never did."

"So what do we do at the top of this hill?" asked Carlie. "Just jump off the lift?"

"Yeah, then you get out of the way so the people behind us don't crash into us. Once we're settled, I'll help you put on your board and we'll get ready to ride."

Whitney slid off the lift with no problem, but Carlie felt clumsy as she clung to her board and scurried to get out of the way. Then Whitney led her off to one side and helped her put on her board. But as soon as Carlie had both feet on the board, she fell down, flat on her face.

Whitney looked like she was trying not to laugh as Carlie slowly struggled to get herself turned around, brushing cold snow from her face and checking to see if her nose was still in place. "Looks like I'm off to a stunning start," she said, and then Whitney did laugh — but not in a mean way. At least that was something.

"Okay, Carlie," said Whitney. "The first rule in riding is that if you feel yourself falling, lean back and fall onto your rear end — not your face. That way it doesn't hurt nearly as much." Then Whitney actually demonstrated this move, planting her bottom into the snow. "Like this. And see ..." she used her hands to push herself upright, "then you can get back up." She pointed to a rider over on a different slope who had just fallen down. "See that guy in khaki over there? Watch as he gets right back up. See how he squats really low, how he uses his hands to kind of guide him along until he gets his balance again."

Carlie nodded, shaking snow out of her hair and trying to regain some confidence. "It looks simple enough."

"It really is, once you get the hang of it." Whitney stood now, spreading her arms as if to balance herself and then bending at her waist and knees. "See, like this, Carlie. It's all about balance, just like on a skateboard. And you have to expect to fall down sometimes. Just try not to do another face-plant." Whitney slapped her backside. "This is much softer. Okay, want me to go first so you can kind of watch and try to imitate me?"

"Sounds good." Carlie stood up, carefully bending her knees and holding her arms out for balance — just like Whitney. She couldn't believe how nice this girl was being — how patient. Carlie had obviously been wrong about her.

"Here I go," said Whitney, slowly taking off. She wove back and forth down the slight incline of the bunny hill, pausing to look back and to make sure that Carlie was still upright. But about midway down, Carlie fell. Fortunately she must've remembered what Whitney said because she fell backward. Then she got up and kept going. She fell once more. This time it was kind of sideways, but she still got back up and rode the rest of the way down without another spill.

"Not bad," said Whitney.

"Really?" Carlie adjusted her goggles.

"Yeah, I think there's hope for you yet."

"That was pretty fun," said Carlie with enthusiasm. "Well, other than the falling part."

"How's it going?" asked Amy as she and Chelsea came and stopped beside them. Carlie was surprised to see that Amy was managing fairly well.

"Amy's catching on," admitted Chelsea. "Who'd of thunk?"

Amy grinned. "Yeah, it's not that hard. It's about balance."

"Right," said Carlie, feeling a little discouraged now.

"I didn't even fall down on the bunny hill," bragged Amy. "And Chelsea fell down once."

"That's only because I was watching you," said Chelsea. Then she laughed. "Don't worry about Amy, I think she's going to be a natural."

Carlie frowned. "I fell down like three times already."

"Maybe you should try skiing," suggested Amy.

"Not yet," said Whitney, tugging on Carlie's arm. "One run is too soon to give up. Time to go again."

"Let's do the bunny hill again too," Chelsea said to Amy. "And if you don't fall down, maybe we can try a longer slope."

"What do you mean if I don't fall down?" said Amy defensively. "You're the one who fell down."

"Fine," said Chelsea. "Let's hit the regular slope then."

Now Amy didn't look so sure. "Okay, maybe one more bunny-hill run."

"How about you guys?" asked Chelsea to Carlie. "You going to try a regular slope today?"

"I think I should do the bunny slope a few times first," said Carlie.

"Let's get going," called Chelsea as she led the way toward the bunny-hill lift line with Amy trailing behind her.

"Use your back foot to push yourself along like this," said Whitney, showing Carlie how to propel her board along like the other girls were doing.

Carlie imitated Whitney and discovered that it was actually pretty easy. In a way it was like skateboarding.

"That's good," said Whitney.

"It's not that hard," said Carlie, but still she focused. She really wanted to get this.

"Let's get in line," called Whitney as she glided along. "This time we'll ride up with our boards on, okay?"

"Okay."

It took a bit of doing, and the lift operator had to pause the lift when they got on, but Carlie managed to get on with her board still attached to her foot. "Getting off can be tricky," warned Whitney. "Just make sure you keep your board pointing straight ahead, and use that back foot to keep it going straight. You think you can do that?"

"I think I can, I think I can, I think I can."

Whitney laughed. "You sound like the Little Blue Engine."

"I know." Carlie kept looking straight ahead. "I'm trying to think positively."

Carlie's positive thinking appeared to be working because she got off the lift without any problem.

"Wow," said Whitney. "I'm actually impressed."

"Lead the way," said Carlie with a pleased grin.

This time they made it down the hill with only one tumble, and this time Carlie landed nicely on her behind and got back up in the same motion. Whitney yelled and cheered for her, slapping her on the back when she got to the bottom of the hill. "That was awesome, Carlie. You're getting it."

"Thanks," said Carlie. "You're a patient teacher."

Whitney just shrugged.

"So, are you guys ready to try a bigger hill now?" asked Chelsea with a slightly impatient tone.

"Not yet," said Whitney. "I want Carlie to take one more run on this chair."

"That sounds like a good idea," said Amy. "Me too. I took a pretty good fall on that last run."

Chelsea groaned. "This bunny hill is so lame." She pointed to a group of little kids who were beginners too. "We look so juvenile."

"Just one more time," said Carlie.

"Whatever." Chelsea just shook her head then took off ahead of them and got into line.

Soon they were all down at the bottom of the hill again. And this time no one fell down.

Amy actually slapped Carlie on the back. "Hey, I think we're doing pretty good for beginners," she said. "Maybe we won't need the beginner's class tomorrow after all."

"So, can we hit a *real* slope now?" demanded Chelsea as she pulled her hat down over her brow and frowned at the rest of them.

"Okay," said Carlie confidently. "Let's go for it, girls."

"Are you sure, Carlie?" asked Whitney.

"Sure, I'm sure."

Of course, once Carlie got off of the "real" lift and saw the big, tall white slope looming down in front of her, she wasn't so sure.

"It's okay," said Whitney, "you can do this."

Carlie peered curiously at her new friend. "How do you know that?"

Whitney grinned. "I can just tell. As soon as I saw you I thought you were a girl who could take on an adventure."

Carlie smiled now. "Yeah," she said. "I am." Feeling confident and good, she started her first ride down the mountain. As long as she stayed focused and slightly relaxed, she managed to do fairly well. It was when she doubted herself that she usually fell. But at least she fell on her bottom now, and more and more she would pop back up and continue. Riding was turning out to be totally cool, and at this rate Carlie expected to be as good as the best after a couple more days.

"Woo-hoo!" she hooted as she took off on her sixth run down the "real" slope. This time she made it all the way down without falling once — a record for her.

"You're doing great," Whitney told Carlie as they rode up for what everyone agreed would be the last time.

"You're a great teacher," said Carlie.

"And you're a good learner."

"Thanks."

chapter five

By the end of the day, Carlie felt a little bit sore, but mostly she felt really, really good. She could tell she'd gotten a lot better. "I can't wait to go again tomorrow," she told Whitney as they carried their boards back to their cabin.

"Well, you're doing great," said Whitney. "I'm sure you'll be an old pro by the time we go home."

Morgan and Emily were walking with them, and just as they reached the turnoff to the cabin, Chelsea and Amy joined them too. But no one was walking too fast.

"Man, am I starved," said Morgan as they stopped in front of their cabin, taking turns putting their boards into the racks by the door.

"Me too," said Carlie as she stomped the snow off her boots. "Too bad dinner isn't for like an hour."

"Gives us time to do some primping," said Amy.

"*I'm* not primping," declared Carlie.

"Me neither," said Morgan.

"Why not?" Whitney peered curiously at her now.

"Why should I?" asked Carlie.

"Don't you want to look pretty?" demanded Amy.

Carlie laughed. "Not only do I *not* want to look pretty, I might not even take a shower."

"Eeuw!" Amy pinched her fingers over her nose. "Nasty!"

But Carlie just laughed. "This is supposed to be like a vacation," she said. "I have to clean up all the time at home. I plan to be a total bum here."

"Me too," said Morgan with a grin.

"I'm with them," added Emily. "Let's go slumming, girls."

"No way," said Amy. "I'm not going to walk around looking like a slob."

"You girls are seriously going to let yourselves go when there are guys around to see?" Chelsea looked honestly stunned.

"Why not?" Carlie asked as she flopped onto her bunk and started to remove her boots.

"Yeah, who cares about boys?" said Emily.

Whitney peered curiously at them like she thought they'd either lost their minds or were just pulling her leg. "Yeah, right," she said finally. "You guys don't care about guys. Tell me another one."

"Forget about them," said Chelsea. "Besides, this will keep the bathroom from getting too crowded anyway." And suddenly they were placing dibs on the mirror and making a mad dash to get their primping things and squeezing themselves into the bathroom.

"Save room in there for me," called Amy as she tossed her pink fluffy hat onto her bed and grabbed up her bag.

Emily laughed. "Let them primp until the cows come home," she said as she peeled off her damp parka and slung it over a chair. "I could care less."

"I guess we'll be the three slobs," said Carlie.

"Oh, I don't know," said Morgan. "I might go all out a little later and put on some lip gloss."

"I'm not touching my hair," said Emily as she casually flipped a blonde braid into the air. "These are staying put until I go home."

"I wish my hair was long enough for braids," said Carlie sadly. "All this moisture, and I won't be able to get a brush through these curls."

"So, don't," suggested Morgan. "Just go au naturale. Maybe we can work your hair into dreadlocks."

"Really?" Okay, Carlie didn't even know what dreadlocks were, but if Morgan thought it would be cool, maybe Carlie would try it.

After a while, Chelsea, Whitney, and Amy emerged from the bathroom, complete with makeup and hairstyles that looked just about perfect. Plus, they'd all changed their clothes. Not only that, but it smelled like a perfume counter in the cabin as Chelsea liberally doused herself with something in a pink bottle.

"Is that Pink Sugar cologne?" asked Amy with interest.

"Sure is," said Chelsea.

"Ooh," said Amy. "I love that fragrance."

"Want some?" asked Chelsea, holding out the bottle.

"All right!" Amy laughed as she gave herself a generous squirt.

"What's up with the perfume?" demanded Carlie as she sniffed the air indignantly. "What about the rights of other people's noses?"

"Yeah," said Emily. "And what is up with all this primping anyway?"

"You do seem to be taking this fashion show a little too seriously," agreed Morgan as she tossed a damp sock across the room. "What's up?"

Amy laughed. "Nothing you girls would care about."

"She means boys," said Emily.

"Do you really think boys are going to care that you fixed your hair?" asked Carlie.

"Or put on makeup," added Emily.

Morgan peeled off a second soggy sock. "Seriously, don't you know what kind of guys are on this trip?"

"Cute guys." Amy giggled and smoothed her hand over her already smooth hair.

"Yeah," said Whitney. "That Jeff Sanders is adorable."

"You can have him," said Chelsea. "It's Enrico that I want. Don't you think he looks just like Antonio Banderas?"

"He does," agreed Amy.

"But I get first dibs," said Chelsea.

Carlie tried not to gag as Morgan and Emily ducked into the bathroom.

"I think you girls deserve whatever you get," said Carlie lightly, hoping that might end this stupid conversation.

But now Whitney bent down and looked directly at Carlie, who was still sitting on her bunk. "And, seriously, Carlie, you'll probably be sorry that you're missing out on all the fun."

"Yeah, right." Carlie shook her head and rolled her eyes. "What fun."

"Don't pick on us because we care about our looks," said Amy indignantly. "We can't help it if we don't want to go around like slobs."

"We're heading to the lodge now," said Chelsea lightly. "Amy and I challenged a couple of the boys to a before-dinner pool game."

Carlie frowned at the three of them. *"Why?"*

Amy laughed. "Oh, don't worry, Carlie, *someday* you'll understand."

"When you're older that is," added Chelsea.

Of course, this only aggravated Carlie more. Just because she wasn't thirteen yet didn't mean she didn't understand their stupidity right now. Besides, she was older than Amy. Even so, she wouldn't lower herself to their standards. But it did hurt a bit to see Whitney acting like this after she'd been such a patient snowboard instructor earlier. Carlie had almost started to think that the two of them might become friends. Now she wasn't so sure.

Whitney and Chelsea snickered as they put on their parkas, both with hoods trimmed in white faux fur as if they had planned it, although Carlie knew that wasn't possible since they'd only just met. But perhaps those two girls, and Amy too, were alike. As more girls entered the cabin, the three giggling girls exited, loudly banging the door behind them.

"Did they leave?" asked Emily as she came out of the bathroom.

Carlie stuck her nose in the air and strutted across the cabin with her head slightly cocked and shoulders thrown back. "Yes," she said in a haughty tone. "But don't worry, little girl, *someday* you'll understand why they are such idiots over stupid old boys."

Emily doubled over, laughing so loud that she snorted.

"Don't let them get to you, Carlie," said Morgan, sticking her head out the bathroom now. "They can't help themselves."

"But how rude was that?" demanded Carlie. "What a putdown."

"We all know that Chelsea doesn't always think before she speaks," said Emily. "You have to cut her some slack."

"Yeah," agreed Carlie. She made a face like a dill pickle. "And now Amy is starting to get *boy crazy* too."

"Well, it was bound to happen," said Morgan as she stood in front of the mirror, putting on lip gloss.

"But it's so *stupid.*" said Carlie.

"Not really," said Morgan. "It's just that you're not used to it."

"Don't tell me you're going to be boy crazy too," said Carlie.

Morgan shook her head. "No. But there's nothing we can do about girls who are, Carlie."

"That's true," admitted Emily. "To be fair, some boys are sort of nice."

"No way," said Carlie. "Are you talking about Jeff Sanders? Just because everyone says he likes you, Emily? Are you boy crazy too?"

She just shrugged. "That doesn't mean I'm boy crazy."

"Is everyone in the club turning boy crazy?" moaned Carlie. "Maybe you guys should just kick me out."

"No one is getting kicked out of the club," said Morgan as she pulled a clean hoody sweatshirt over her head.

"What club?" Laura emerged from the bathroom with a toothbrush sticking out of her mouth and white foam coming out one side.

"You're brushing your teeth in the middle of the day?" demanded Carlie in an irritated voice. "What is up with everyone anyway? I'm stuck with a bunch of neat freaks."

"Watch it," said Emily. "They might start calling you Pigpen."

"Well, this is supposed to be a vacation," complained Carlie. "I have to do all that clean and brush and scrub stuff at home. Give me a break."

"What club?" asked Laura again.

"Oh, it's just something we do, back where we live," Morgan barely explained to her.

"Where *do* you live?" asked Laura.

"Harbor View," said Emily as she pulled on a fresh pair of socks.

"Oh, you mean that old trailer park on the edge of town?"

"Yeah, whatever," Morgan glanced at Emily and rolled her eyes. Then she flopped onto her bunk now. "I'm taking a quick nap."

"Me too," said Carlie as she flopped back onto her bunk.

"Aren't you two going to clean up for dinner?" asked Laura.

You mean clean up for the boys? thought Carlie as she closed her eyes. Why bother?

Soon more girls were coming in from the cold, using the bathroom, changing clothes, fixing hair, doing makeup ... basically just primping. Carlie tried to ignore them, but it did bug her some that everyone in this cabin (besides Morgan, Emily, and her) had gotten the weird idea that this ski trip was supposed to be some kind of fashion show. To be fair, it wasn't that Carlie didn't care about her appearance at all. She sort of did, at least some of the time. But this was supposed to be a ski trip. A vacation! If Carlie had wanted to be nagged about how she looked, or if she needed to be reminded to act like a lady, she could've just stayed home.

"Hey, Carlie," said Emily. "Wake up, sleepyhead. Or we'll be late to dinner."

Carlie popped up, taking a moment to remember where she was. "Oh," she said, as she got out of the bunk. "I really dozed off."

"Do you want to clean up at all?" asked Emily.

Carlie scowled at her.

"Okay, okay ..." Emily held up her hands.

"Come on then, Pigpen," teased Morgan as she held out Carlie's parka for her. "Let's go eat."

"Do you think that Whitney really likes Jeff?" asked Emily as they trudged through the snow toward the big lodge.

"Are you worried?" asked Morgan.

Emily shrugged. Then Carlie let out a discouraged sigh. What was happening to all her friends? Were they all turning boy crazy? And, if so, why?

chapter six

"Hey, funny face," said Jeff Sanders as he came up from behind the girls and tugged on one of Emily's braids. Carlie glanced at Emily, curious as to how she would react to this. Would she be glad for the attention? Or would she put the stupid boy in his place?

"Knock it off!" Emily snapped at him, then turned her attention back to the video game that she was playing with Carlie. But Jeff just grinned like it was no big deal. Then, as the girls finished up the game, Carlie turned and glared at the stupid boy. As it figured, Enrico Valdez was with him.

They had all finished dinner a while ago and were hanging out in the games area until eight o'clock, when Cory planned to gather them back in the fireside room for a meeting. Carlie and Emily had nabbed a video game while Morgan stood nearby, waiting in line for a pool table.

"Saw you riding this afternoon," Jeff said to Emily. "You're pretty good."

"Thanks for noticing," said Emily in a cool tone.

"You were pretty good too," Enrico said to Carlie in a quiet tone, like he was unsure of himself.

Carlie studied him for a moment. Was he making fun of her? Still, she didn't want to make a scene. "I'm okay …" She looked away. "For a beginner anyway."

"She's not a beginner anymore," said Whitney from behind. Carlie hadn't even known she was there. "You should've seen her on her last run."

"Hey, I saw you having a good ride today, Whitney," said Jeff. "You look like you know what you're doing."

"She does," said Carlie with more enthusiasm. "She's been teaching me."

Jeff grinned as he jerked his thumb toward Enrico. "Maybe you should give him lessons. 'Cause if you guys wanna see a real beginner you should watch old Enrico ride — it's something to see."

"I did see him," admitted Carlie. "I saw him splattering himself all over the slope about halfway down the red chair."

Jeff laughed. "Man, was that ever a yard sale."

Enrico rubbed his elbow and looked slightly embarrassed. "Kinda painful too."

"Don't feel bad," Morgan assured him. "I had a few good wrecks myself today."

"But she's definitely improving," said Emily.

"Hey, you guys wanna shoot some pool with us?" asked Jeff as one of the pool tables suddenly opened up.

"Sure," said Whitney, stepping up and picking up a cue.

Suddenly Carlie was unsure. Who were they inviting

to play? And hadn't Morgan been trying to get a table for the girls? What now?

"Girls against guys," challenged Whitney.

"You're on," agreed Jeff as he picked up a cue, holding it out to Emily with a smile.

"You guys go ahead," said Emily as she grabbed Morgan's arm and tugged her away. "Let's go play a video game."

And before Carlie could protest, she suddenly found herself partnered with Whitney again. And before she could think of an excuse to get away, Jeff and Enrico were putting billiard balls into the triangle. And then the four of them were playing pool, like no big deal. How on earth did that happen? How was it that Carlie Garcia, after all her little speeches against stupid boy-crazy girls, was suddenly stuck with Jeff Sanders and Enrico Valdez?

They were several minutes into the game when Carlie noticed Chelsea and Amy sauntering up to the pool table.

"Hey, guys," said Chelsea in a friendly tone. "How come we weren't invited to play?"

"Because you weren't here?" ventured Carlie. Her nose was starting to twitch now and judging by the smell, Amy and Chelsea had both just applied another dose of that stinky pink perfume. Carlie also noticed that they both had on a fresh layer of lip gloss as well. What were they trying to prove anyway?

"What's that smell?" asked Jeff as he stood up from making a corner pocket shot.

Chelsea giggled. "You mean that stinky sweaty smell, like someone forgot to take a shower today?" She glanced directly at Carlie now.

"No, I mean that smell like a funeral parlor full of rotten flowers," said Jeff as he bent down to gauge his next shot.

"That just shows how much you know," said Chelsea in a slightly offended tone.

"So, who's winning?" asked Amy.

"Right now we are," said Whitney.

"Not for long," said Enrico as Jeff sunk another shot.

"Good one," admitted Carlie. "But you can stop right there, Mister."

"You're playing girls against boys?" said Chelsea. "Where's the fun in that?"

"The fun is when we whoop them," said Whitney as Jeff finally missed a shot. "Okay, Carlie, we need you to make this. Put one in for the girls."

Carlie held her breath as she lined up her shot, and to everyone's surprise (mostly hers), she not only got one ball in the pocket but a second one as well. "Woo-hoo!" she shouted.

"Way to go," said Whitney, giving her a high five.

"Not bad," said Enrico with real admiration.

"Yeah," agreed Jeff. "The girl not only snowboards like a guy, but she shoots pool like a guy too."

Chelsea just shook her head. "Poor thing *smells* like a guy too."

Carlie took in a quick breath, but decided not to let her irritation show.

But suddenly Whitney was glaring at Chelsea. "That wasn't a very nice thing to say."

Chelsea just shrugged. "I was just kidding."

"Yeah," said Amy. "You shouldn't take things so seriously."

Then to Carlie's stunned surprise, Enrico leaned over and picked up one of her curls between his thumb and forefinger and actually took a big loud sniff of it. She glared at him, unsure as to whether she should slap him or just walk off. But instead she braced herself and got ready for even more teasing.

But Enrico just smiled. "I think she smells pretty good — for a girl anyway." Then they all laughed, and the four returned to their pool game.

"What's with some girls?" asked Enrico as Chelsea and Amy walked away.

"It's like they wanna start a fight over nothing," said Jeff as Enrico missed his next shot.

"Oh, I don't think they want to fight," said Whitney as she chalked her cue and studied the table for her turn.

"They just want attention ..." said Carlie. "From you guys."

"Well, they should act more like one of the guys," said Jeff.

Carlie considered this as they continued to play. To be honest, it really wasn't that bad hanging with the boys when you could just be one of the guys. In some ways it was better than being with Chelsea and Amy when they were acting boy crazy. She wondered why some girls wanted to complicate things. What was the point in fixing yourself all up, putting on perfume, and then acting the way they did? Then she considered Whitney ... she had been acting kind of boy crazy earlier, but now she seemed fairly normal. Although, here they were hanging with boys. That wasn't exactly normal. Suddenly Carlie felt confused.

"Your shot, Carlie," said Jeff.

"And you could win the game if you sink it," said Whitney.

Carlie focused on the table now. Her dad was the one who had taught her to play pool. They'd played a lot of games on Tio Geraldo's table. She tried to remember all the tips her dad had given her. In some ways it wasn't much different than what she'd been telling herself about snowboarding. Focus and then relax. And so she did.

"Great shot!" exclaimed Enrico as the eight ball went straight into the side pocket just like she had called it.

"Woo-hoo!" said Whitney, hugging Carlie. "Girls rule!"

"Think you girls can do that again?" asked Jeff.

"Don't know why not," said Carlie.

"Best two out of three?" asked Enrico.

Carlie glanced over to see if Morgan and Emily were around. Maybe it should be their turn to play. But both girls had disappeared. And, no way did Carlie want to surrender this game to Amy and Chelsea, although they were watching from over by the video games.

"You're on!" said Carlie.

"Hey, have you guys tried the half-pipe yet?" asked Jeff as they racked up the balls for the next game.

"What's that like?" asked Carlie. "I mean, I've skateboarded on a half-pipe before, but it was made out of plywood."

"It's like a giant half-pipe that's made out of snow and ice," explained Enrico.

"Pretty much the same concept as a skateboard half-pipe," said Jeff.

"Only a whole lot bigger," added Whitney.

"And you can do jumps and things," said Jeff.

"If you know how," added Enrico with a sheepish grin. "Not that I have any problems with that myself."

"I'm gonna try it out tomorrow," said Jeff.

"That sounds fun," said Whitney as Chelsea and

Amy came back to stand by the pool table again. "I sort of attempted a couple of pretty lame jumps today, but I couldn't get much — "

"You were great," said Carlie. "One time you must've been close to a foot in the air."

"You were doing jumps?" said Chelsea with a skeptical expression.

"Not very good ones," said Whitney. "And Carlie did a couple of jumps too."

"I tried," admitted Carlie.

"Hey, you guys should come to the half-pipe tomorrow," Jeff said more to Whitney than the others.

"You should come too," said Enrico with his eyes on Carlie. "Maybe you guys can help me."

"I know how to jump too," said Chelsea.

"Why don't we all go?" said Amy.

"Sure," said Jeff. "Why not?"

"Although I just plan to watch," said Amy. "I'm not ready to do any jumping yet."

"I wouldn't mind trying the half-pipe," mused Carlie. She remembered some of the stunts she used to do on the skateboard. Maybe it wouldn't be that much different. At least if she fell the snow would be better than plywood and cement.

"I want to try it too," said Chelsea. "I caught some air myself today."

"And I'll come to watch," said Amy eagerly.

"Why don't we meet there, like say, around eleven?" suggested Jeff.

"Sounds good," said Enrico. "That'll give everyone some time to get warmed up." He chuckled. "And get our nerve up too."

"It's a date," said Chelsea, acting as if the guys had invited her personally. Was she aware that she'd pretty much invited herself?

Carlie controlled herself from rolling her eyes.

"You guys are coming too?" Jeff directed this to her and Whitney.

"Sure," said Carlie. "I'd like to check it out."

"Tell Emily and Morgan too," said Jeff in an off-handed way. But something about his expression made Carlie think that he especially wanted Emily to come. Still, if that was the case, why was he being so friendly to Whitney? Finally, Carlie decided not to think about such dumb things. It was ruining her game. And, as they continued to play, the boys won the second game.

"Our turn now," said Chelsea as she started to put the balls back on the table.

"Not yet," said Jeff. "We're playing best two out of three, and at the moment it's a tie."

Chelsea frowned. "That's not fair."

"I know," said Carlie. "And since we were playing

girls against guys, we could let Chelsea and Amy replace the girl team." She winked at Whitney. "That is, if you don't mind."

Whitney looked slightly disappointed, but simply shrugged. "Fine with me."

So Carlie and Whitney handed their pool cues over to Chelsea and Amy, who looked surprised but pleased. The boys looked slightly disappointed. And for some unexplainable reason, this made Carlie very happy.

"Good luck, girls," she said.

"Yeah," said Whitney. "We're counting on you to win this thing for the girls."

"Thanks," said Chelsea. "We won't let you down."

"Wanna get a soda?" asked Carlie as she picked up her parka.

"Sounds good to me," said Whitney.

"See ya, Whitney," called Jeff as they walked away.

"See ya, Carlie," called Enrico.

"I think Jeff likes you," Carlie said as they went to the soda machine and filled their cups with ice. She almost added that she thought he liked Emily too, but wasn't sure if that would sound right.

"And I think Enrico likes you." Whitney chuckled. "And that should make Chelsea good and mad since she really likes Enrico."

Carlie shrugged. "Oh, I think the boys just consider us to be like one of the guys. Ya know?"

Whitney laughed. "Hey, that works for me."

"Totally."

"So, are you as boy crazy as Amy and Chelsea?" asked Carlie.

"Nah, I just know how to play along."

Carlie sighed. "That's a relief."

"You should learn to play along too, Carlie. It's much easier than fighting with everyone."

"I don't know ... all that primping and stuff ... I can live without it."

"Apparently the boys agree with you."

"How'd the pool game with the boys go?" said Emily as she and Morgan joined Carlie and Whitney at the café.

"Okay," said Carlie. "But why did you guys take off like that?"

"It looked like you had enough people to play," said Emily.

Morgan peered closely at Carlie now. "So, what was up with you making such a big deal about hating boys and all that."

"I never said I hated boys," said Carlie. "I just don't get all that primping and perfume stuff."

"Seems like the boys don't get it either," pointed out Whitney. Then she told Emily and Morgan about how they hadn't cared for the smell of the perfume. And then they all laughed.

"I think it's better when you're just *one of the guys*," Carlie said.

Whitney nodded. "Yeah. Like it's no big deal."

"Oh, yeah," said Carlie. Then she told them about the plan to meet at the half-pipe tomorrow.

"Cool," said Emily. "I've been wanting to try it."

"So has Chelsea," said Whitney.

"Speaking of Chelsea," said Emily. "You should've heard her going on about Carlie and Enrico. She was so jealous. She acted like you guys were about to run off and get married or something."

Carlie burst into loud laughter. "Yeah, right!"

"Speaking of jealous," said Whitney in a careful tone. "I think Jeff is really nice, Emily. But I heard that maybe you and he like — "

"No way," said Emily quickly. "Jeff is a nice guy. But he and I are — well, nothing." She laughed nervously. "And that's just how I want to keep it."

Morgan reached up and gave her a high five. "Emily and I just had a long talk," she said. "We both decided we are way too young to get serious about boys."

"That's right," said Emily. Then she peered curiously at Carlie.

"So am I," said Carlie quickly. "You know that, don't you?"

Morgan nodded and patted Carlie on the back. "Yeah. That's what we thought."

Carlie sighed in relief. And then it was time to meet in the fireside room. Carlie sat between Morgan and Whitney, right in the front row. Although she felt sleepy, she really tried to focus in on what Cory, the youth pastor, was saying. It seemed to be tied into Christmas and had to do with forgiving people. But a lot of it seemed to be floating around her head, and she couldn't quite make it all out. Cory was saying how God's forgiveness was supposed to teach them how to forgive other people. Somehow it was all connected like a circle. But Carlie was so tired that it seemed like that circle was spinning and making her dizzy.

Cory spoke a little more and then finally gave an invitation for anyone in the group who hadn't fully received God's forgiveness to do so — and a couple of kids raised their hands. Carlie wondered if she should too, but then she knew she'd made a commitment to Jesus last summer and she'd been trying to honor it — as much as she knew how to anyway. So she thought she was probably okay. But then Cory invited them to use this time to forgive others. Now Carlie wasn't really sure what to do about that. She didn't completely understand this forgiveness thing. For one thing, she still felt a little grumpy toward her mom. Besides that, she wasn't too happy with Chelsea. But did that mean she needed to forgive them? And, if so, why should she? If anything, it seemed like they should do something to make her feel better. And, really, what did it matter whether she forgave them or not — especially if no one knew about it.

After the meeting ended, they were all invited to hang out for cocoa and snacks or to return to their cabins to hit the hay. As Carlie sipped some cocoa, she noticed that Jeff and Enrico were back at the pool table again, playing another game, this time with Chelsea and Whitney. And just as Carlie looked up, she saw Chelsea standing inches from Enrico, smiling at him like she wanted to kiss him or something equally gross. Still, it wasn't like Carlie cared. Why should she? Let Chelsea make a total fool of herself. Let Enrico too. Why should she care?

"I'm sleepy," said Morgan.

"Me too," admitted Carlie.

"Me three," said Emily.

"Where are Amy and Chelsea?" asked Morgan.

Carlie pointed over to the pool table area where Amy was flitting about the foursome who were still playing pool.

Emily groaned. "It figures. I hear Chelsea's not the only one who thinks Enrico is cute."

Carlie laughed. "Boy crazy!"

"It's like a disease," said Emily, nodding over to where Taylor and Cassie appeared to be obviously flirting with two other boys from the youth group.

"Let's get out of here before we catch it too," said Carlie. Then, laughing loudly, the three girls made a quick and noisy exit.

But later on, when the cabin was dark and quiet, and everyone seemed to be asleep, Carlie was still awake. She was thinking about the events of the evening. Suddenly, she thought maybe it was too late for her — maybe she had already caught that deadly disease. Not that she was boy crazy. She most certainly was not. But, at the same time, she had an uncomfortable feeling toward Chelsea — especially as she remembered how Chelsea had been cozying up to Enrico during that last pool game. She was afraid it might be jealousy and somehow related to Enrico. But that made no sense. Carlie had no interest in Enrico ... well, other than joking around with him, beating him at pool, and being "one of the guys." Surely that wasn't the same as being boy crazy. And that was exactly what she told herself as she drifted off to sleep.

chapter seven

The next morning, Whitney and Carlie hit the slopes right after breakfast. They both wanted to get in lots of rides before they went to meet everyone at the half-pipe. Carlie's confidence increased as she practiced a few jumps during her runs. It really wasn't that different from skateboarding. More and more, she realized she was pretty good at this. She knew how to catch air! But she also knew how to fall. And her last fall, although she landed on her backside, was a hard one. She was afraid she'd have the bruises to prove it. Still, she was having fun. That's what mattered!

"You're looking awesome with your jumps," Whitney told her as they rode the red chair up again.

"You are too," said Carlie.

Whitney laughed. "Well, at least I only fell down twice on that last run. That wasn't too bad."

"I fell down more than that," admitted Carlie. "But no face-plants."

"So, are you ready for the half-pipe?"

"Sure. It'll be fun. How about you?"

Carlie shrugged, still remembering that last fall. "Yeah, I guess so."

"You know, you shouldn't do it if you don't feel sure. I remember an instructor told me once that it was all about confidence."

"I know." Carlie nodded.

"You have to believe in yourself."

"Just like the Little Blue Engine."

Whitney laughed. "Exactly."

"Well, I think I can, I think I can, I think I can."

And after Carlie did a few more jumps, with no falls, even taking on some small moguls, her confidence returned. By the time they reached the bottom of the slope, she really did feel sure of herself. "It's almost eleven," she announced.

"To the half-pipe," said Whitney as she pushed off with her back foot. Carlie followed, keeping up with no problems. She could hardly believe that yesterday was her first time doing this. But then Carlie had always been a good athlete. Plus, she'd been good on a skateboard. Why shouldn't she be good at this?

"Hey," said Jeff as Whitney and Carlie joined the rest of them at the foot of the half-pipe. "You guys just missed Enrico's big wipeout."

"And he was actually doing pretty well too," said Chelsea.

"You should've seen how high he got," added Amy.

Enrico groaned. "What goes up … must come down."

"I thought you were going to pass on the pipe," said Whitney.

"He changed his mind." Jeff chuckled.

"Too bad," said Carlie.

"Well, you can't get better if you don't try," said Enrico.

"Not me," said Morgan as she planted her snowboard in the snow then flopped down beside it. "I am officially a spectator."

"You and me both," said Amy as she sat down beside her.

"I'm going up," announced Emily.

"All right," said Jeff.

"Me too," said Chelsea. "I can't wait to try this. Anyone else coming?"

"I don't know," said Whitney, frowning up at the enormous half tube of hard-packed snow. "It looks kinda scary from down here."

"It's better once you get up there," said Enrico.

"That from a guy who just wiped out?"

"Hey, I was trying too hard," he said. "Next time will be better."

"How about you, Carlie?" challenged Chelsea. "I'll bet you want to pass on this too."

"I'm in," said Carlie.

Enrico grinned at her. "Good for you."

"You coming, Whitney?" asked Carlie.

Whitney studied the steeply sloped sides of the half-pipe then slowly nodded. "I guess so ..."

"Hey, you guys," said Morgan with concern. "Do you think you should be wearing helmets?"

Carlie had noticed that several of the kids were wearing helmets, but those were kids who were doing some pretty fancy tricks too. "I don't know about the others," called Carlie. "But I won't be doing anything too risky."

"We'll be fine," Whitney assured her.

"Everybody ready?" asked Jeff as he picked up his board to lead the way.

"I am," announced Whitney as she followed right behind him. Then Emily followed her, and Carlie and Enrico and Chelsea brought up the rear. When they finally got to the end of the line, Carlie just watched as other kids took their turns. She saw that some of them, like her, were probably new to this. And many of them were taking it pretty carefully. That was what she planned to do. No jumping for her. At least not on the first run. She knew she'd be doing good just to make some clean turns and get a feel for the half-pipe first. Maybe she wouldn't jump at all. No one could make her.

"Nervous?" asked Enrico quietly.

Carlie had almost forgotten he was behind her. "A little," she admitted.

"Me too."

"I'm not," said Chelsea. "I think this will be fun."

"Who wants to go first?" asked Jeff as they made their way to the front of the line.

"Maybe ladies should go first," offered Enrico.

"Why?" challenged Carlie. "Are you scared?"

"No way," said Enrico. "Just being polite."

"Why don't you go first, Carlie," urged Chelsea, stepping back next to Enrico so that Carlie could move to the front of the line.

"Okay," said Carlie, deciding to take the challenge. Besides, that way she'd get it over with. She waited for the next rider to go, and then she got into place. She secured her back foot onto the board and took in a slow deep breath.

"But I'm not doing anything fancy," she said as she took off. She put all her energy into simply focusing and relaxing. And just like she said, she didn't do anything fancy. She just rode, did some nice turns, and by the time she reached the end, she felt rather pleased with herself. It was actually pretty fun.

"Way to go, Carlie," called out Morgan from where the spectators were sitting.

"Smooth," yelled Enrico from up on top.

"Thanks." Now Carlie turned to watch Chelsea coming. Her ride was slightly more adventurous than Carlie's. Two times she made it nearly to the edge of the half-pipe before she turned.

"Nice ride," Carlie said to Chelsea when she reached the bottom.

"Thanks," said Chelsea. "I almost did a jump ... I think I will on the next run."

"Whitney's coming now," called Amy. They all turned to watch as Whitney made a somewhat choppy run, nearly falling twice.

"Good job," said Carlie as Whitney joined them.

"I don't know ..." Whitney shook her head. "I'm not feeling too comfortable up there."

"Then don't go again," said Morgan.

Whitney nodded as she took her foot out of the board. "I won't."

"Here comes Jeff," called Chelsea. They all watched as Jeff rode down the half-pipe, actually making a couple of fairly controlled jumps that he landed successfully. They clapped for him, and when he ended his run he had a big grin on his face.

"That was so cool," he said. "Here comes Emily."

"Be careful, Em," called Morgan quietly. But Emily managed a graceful ride, stopping right in front of them like it was nothing.

"That was great," Morgan told her happily. "I was afraid you were going to kill yourself."

Emily laughed. "Glad you have such confidence in me."

"Sorry."

"Hey, here comes Enrico," called Jeff.

"I hope he doesn't wipe out again," said Amy.

They all watched quietly as Enrico started his run. And not only did he not wipe out, he actually did a great run, even completing a 180 as well as another small jump before he was finished.

"All right," said Jeff as he high-fived his buddy. "That's the way to do it."

"That felt great," said Enrico happily. "I'm ready to go again."

"You girls going up again too?" asked Jeff.

"Not me," said Whitney as she headed over to where Morgan and Amy were sitting. "But I'll cheer for the rest of you."

"I want to go again," said Emily. "But I need to adjust my binding first."

"Here," said Jeff. "Let me help."

"I'm definitely going up," said Chelsea as she stepped right next to Enrico. "And this time I'm jumping too. Enrico inspired me to try even harder."

He gave her a high five. "Awesome." Then he was heading back up the hill with Chelsea right on his heels.

For some reason this irritated Carlie as she trudged up the hill behind the two of them. Jeff and Emily were still at the bottom, adjusting her bindings, but now Carlie wished she'd waited for them. At least then she wouldn't have to be stuck up here watching Chelsea shamelessly flirting with Enrico — at least that's what it looked like to Carlie.

As they waited in line at the top, Chelsea started to brag about how she was going to jump this time. "I'll bet I catch even more air than you, Enrico."

"No way," he shot back at her. "I'm going even higher on this run."

Chelsea turned and looked at Carlie now. "How about you? Are you going to jump this time?"

"I don't know ..." Carlie looked down the half-pipe as a more experienced rider preformed a slightly clumsy one-and- a-half jump, landing it backward and sliding down without a hitch. But the next rider, a girl, attempted a jump and totally wiped out, face-first. Fortunately, she had on a helmet.

"Oh!" exclaimed Carlie. "That must've hurt."

"Yeah," said Enrico. "You need to be careful."

"And, don't jump if you're scared," said Chelsea in a tone that sounded slightly snooty and superior. "That's the worst thing to do, you know."

Carlie stuck her chin out. "I am not scared."

"Well, you seem sort of uneasy."

"I am not uneasy," said Carlie. "I just haven't decided whether or not I want to jump yet." Of course, as soon as she said this, she knew it sounded silly.

Then Chelsea adjusted her goggles and smiled at Enrico. "I think poor little Carlie is getting freaked."

"I am not freaked."

"Seriously, Carlie," said Enrico. "Don't jump if it doesn't feel good." He was getting ready to go first this time.

Chelsea nodded in what seemed a smug way. "Yeah, Carlie, you should just take it easy." Then they both watched as Enrico made another nice ride. He attempted an even bigger jump this time and almost lost his balance, but caught himself with one hand and made it down without a fall. Their friends at the bottom cheered.

"Here I go," said Chelsea. She took off and rode even higher up the half-pipe this time, making a nice turn, then another, and finally on her third time up she made a jump, twisting in the air to turn back around. Carlie watched with wide eyes, and then Chelsea landed it, her board cutting into the hard-packed snow as if she'd been doing this for years. Then she glided down to where Enrico was waiting. Carlie watched as Enrico gave her a high five, which Chelsea turned into a hug. And suddenly Carlie really did feel jealous.

"Your turn," yelled the guy behind her.

Carlie hurried to get into position, noticing that

Jeff and Emily were in line now. Emily was giving her a thumbs-up.

"Come on, Carlie," yelled Chelsea from the bottom. "Try and beat my run if you can!"

Carlie nodded and took off down the half-pipe. Whether she meant to or not, she felt herself imitating Chelsea's run, riding high up the left side, making a turn, then doing it again on the right. Then she started on the left again, but suddenly she wasn't sure she really wanted to attempt a jump. Yet in that same split-second, she saw the image of Chelsea celebrating down at the bottom, and Carlie knew she at least had to try.

Carlie ducked down low, arms spread, as she used her weight to propel her body upward. Going clear to the edge again, this time the end of her board just clearing it, she sailed into the air. She was so low she could almost touch the tip of her board, and then she turned — perfectly. It was a great moment, almost like flying. And then, just as she was coming down again, her board tilted ever so slightly, the tip biting into the icy surface. Suddenly everything changed. All she could see was the packed snow coming straight at her, and she knew she was going down — face-first, not on her backside like Whitney had taught her to do. Blocking her fall with her right arm, she felt her body twist and heard a snapping sound, like a branch breaking. After that it was all a white blur. A painful white blur.

chapter eight

Somehow Carlie managed to slide down to the bottom of the half-pipe on her side, cradling her injured arm with her right hand. But as her friends gathered around her, hot tears were stinging in her eyes.

"Oh, Carlie!" cried Morgan.

"Are you okay?" asked Emily.

Carlie bit her lip and tried to answer them, but the pain was too intense.

Amy put her hand on Carlie's shoulder. "It's okay to cry," she said quietly.

Just then Chelsea came over. "I *told* you not to jump," she said, reaching down to pull her up.

"No!" cried Carlie. "Don't help me. Please, don't touch me. I hurt my arm. I think it's broken."

Chelsea looked skeptical. "I doubt that you could have broken it just like that, Carlie. You barely even fell." She reached out her hand again, and Carlie cringed, drawing away from her.

"Don't move her," said Morgan.

"I'll go get help," said Emily, taking off in a run toward the lodge.

Before long a crowd gathered around Carlie, making her feel sillier than ever. But soon the ski patrol arrived, and she was gently loaded into a basket sort of thing and transported toward the lodge. If she hadn't been in so much pain, she would've been really embarrassed by all the fuss. As it was, she felt pretty stupid for falling like that, and it didn't help matters to overhear Chelsea acting like she was faking a broken bone just to get everyone's attention. Carlie was relieved that only Morgan and Emily came down to the lodge clinic with her.

"Emily, you stay here with Carlie," instructed Morgan. "And I'll go find Cory or Janna."

After an examination by a tall, blond lodge paramedic named Andre, it was decided that Carlie should be taken to the nearby town. "I'll wrap it in a brace for now," he told her with a bright smile. "But the doc in town will probably do an x-ray, set it, and then put a real cast on." He winked at her. "And then you can get all your boyfriends to sign it for you."

"Yeah ... right ..." Carlie rolled her eyes then took in a deep breath as Andre continued to wrap her arm. It hurt each time he moved it, but Carlie didn't want to show it. She wanted to be brave.

"Hey, a pretty girl like you must have lots of boyfriends," he teased.

"There's one boy who really likes her," said Emily

quietly. She smiled at Carlie as she held onto her good hand. She'd been with Carlie throughout the examination, calmly standing by. Carlie was thankful Emily was there.

"I'll bet there's more than just one," said Andre.

"Hey, Carlie," called Morgan from out in the office area. "I've got Janna here."

"Come in if you want," said Andre. "We're almost done."

"Oh, poor Carlie," said Janna as she came in and gently put an arm around her shoulders. "Does it hurt much?"

"A little," Carlie admitted.

Andre turned to Janna. "I'm afraid it's broken," he said. "But she'll need to go to Arrowhead to see a doctor. We already called ahead. Can you drive her there?"

"No problem." Janna frowned slightly. "You don't think she needs to go to a hospital?"

"That's an option," he said. "But the closest one is an hour away, and I've heard of people waiting in the emergency room for up to three hours. Dr. Ferris is good, and her clinic is fully equipped. We usually send all our less serious injuries her way."

"Sounds good," said Janna. "I just tried to call your mom, Carlie, but no one seems to be home."

Carlie nodded. "She's probably out getting groceries or something." Actually, Carlie felt relieved. She wasn't eager for Mom to hear about this. "But she'll probably be home for sure around two since that's when my little brothers take their naps."

"Well, are you ready to go?" asked Janna.

"I guess." Carlie looked down at her neatly wrapped arm then up at Morgan and Emily. "But you guys don't need to go."

"We want to," said Emily.

Carlie considered this. "That's really sweet, but I already feel bad for spoiling your day. I don't want to spoil the whole ski trip. Why don't you guys just stay here and do a few more runs — do it for me."

"But Carlie, we — "

"Seriously," insisted Carlie. "I'll feel better if I know you guys are back here having fun." Finally they agreed, and then Janna drove Carlie the ten-minute drive to Arrowhead. They went to Dr. Ferris's clinic, and Andre's suspicion was confirmed. Carlie's arm was broken. She tried not to cry as the doctor set the arm back into place, but that actually hurt as badly as when she'd broken it. By the time the doctor finished, there were silent tears slipping down both of Carlie's cheeks.

"It's okay," said Janna softly as she dabbed Carlie's face with a tissue. "Go ahead and cry."

"It hurts," muttered Carlie.

"I know," said Janna. "I broke my arm once too." Then, as the doctor and nurse wrapped the cast material around Carlie's arm, Janna told Carlie about how she'd fallen from a horse when she was eleven. "My arm was just hanging," said Janna. "But I was about a mile from the house. So I just had to hold the broken arm with my good hand and walk all the way back home."

"Wow, that must've really hurt."

"It did. I walked into the kitchen and saw my mom and *bam* — it was like the lights went out. They told me later that I fainted. At first my mom had no idea what was wrong. But when I came to I told her I'd broken my arm. And she didn't believe me! She thought I was saying I broke my arm when I fainted, and she didn't think that was possible. Then I explained about falling off the horse, and she took me to the doctor."

Carlie nodded. "Chelsea didn't believe me either."

"When you broke your arm?"

"She thought I was faking ..." Carlie sniffed. "Just because I was embarrassed that I fell on the half-pipe."

"Girls can be mean," said Janna.

"It's true," said Carlie. "I was embarrassed, but I wasn't faking."

Janna patted her back. "We know ..."

"How does that feel?" asked Dr. Ferris.

"It's okay," she told her, although tears were still coming down her cheeks, and her arm still hurt — but not as much. Now she knew she was crying because she was getting worried about how much this medical treatment was going to cost. She knew that doctors were expensive, and she knew just as well that her family didn't have health insurance. It was a point that her mother often made. So now, not only would Mom freak over a broken bone, she would be worried about money too. And it was all Carlie's fault. She shouldn't have taken that jump. And all because she wanted to compete with Chelsea. How stupid!

Carlie wondered how much this broken arm was going to cost her family. She wondered if she should've done something differently. But it wasn't like she could've asked the doctor for the "cheap" bone-setting plan, and she doubted that they would've let her pass on the cast. What was done was done.

"How's that?" asked Dr. Ferris as she adjusted a sling around the cast.

Carlie looked down at the strange-looking arm and sighed. "Fine."

Then Janna went out to the waiting room to speak to the receptionist, and the nurse checked some other things like Carlie's temperature and blood pressure. Then she had Carlie take a couple of nonprescription pain pills and gave her samples for more. "Take these every four to six hours if you need to," she told her. "And Dr. Ferris will give you one pill for tonight to help you sleep. But you should probably make an appointment with your family doctor when you get home."

"Thanks." Even as Carlie said this she wondered how much more it would cost to go to the doctor again. Just getting her school physical had been expensive. She remembered Mom complaining about not having insurance then.

"How are you doing?" asked Janna when Carlie came back out to the waiting area.

Carlie forced a smile. "I've had better days."

"I just tried to call your mom again," Janna told her. "But she still wasn't home, and I hated to leave a message and get her all worried."

"Thanks for not doing that — she probably would've freaked." She hated to imagine her mom's reaction to hearing a message that Carlie had broken her arm. Hadn't Mom made her promise not to break anything? But how do you keep a promise like that?

"Are you sure there's no one else I can call?" asked Janna as she put Carlie's parka over her shoulders.

Carlie considered Tia Maria, but for the moment she didn't want anyone in her family to know what had happened. "No ..."

Janna frowned. "I'm not sure what we should do. I could drive you back to town and — "

"No," said Carlie suddenly. "I don't want to go back."

"But, aren't you in pain?"

"It's not that bad," said Carlie as she forced a smile. "Can't I stay for the rest of the snow trip?"

"You don't want to go home?"

"Not yet," said Carlie. Now she started to cry again. She wasn't even sure why, but it was probably a combination of everything — the sadness that she wouldn't get to snowboard anymore, the fear of how Mom would react to the news, and the concern over the medical expenses. It was all too much.

"What do you want to do, Carlie?" asked Janna kindly.

"Can't I just stay until the end of the trip?"

"I don't know for sure," said Janna. "We really need to talk to your parents and get their permission."

"Can't I call Mom later? I mean, from the lodge?"

"I guess so. Do you want your parents to come pick you up there?" asked Janna.

Carlie frowned, still thinking about everything. "Well, Mom would have to bring my little brothers with her, and it is their nap time. And Dad's out on the fishing boat. It might be kind of inconvenient."

"You don't really want to stick around until the end of the ski trip, do you?"

Carlie smiled hopefully. "Would it be okay if I did?"

"I guess so," said Janna. "I mean, of course, it's okay with me. Just as long as your parents are okay with it. And as long as you feel okay."

Carlie looked down at her cast and sighed. "I obviously won't be able to snowboard."

"No ..." Janna shook her head. "But you can hang out in the lodge and sit by the fireplace and drink cocoa." She grinned. "Like the girls in those old movies — you know the ones who really don't want to ski anyway."

"Yeah ..." Carlie frowned. "Except that I really do want to ... snowboard I mean."

"Well, that's not going to happen." Janna firmly shook her head.

"But at least I could see my friends."

"And you could read books," suggested Janna. "I saw a bookshelf in the lodge."

"And I could attend the meetings and stuff," said Carlie hopefully. "I mean, it would be better than just sitting at home."

"As long as you're not in pain."

"That way I can get my money's worth for the trip," said Carlie. "I mean, since I paid for the whole thing ... shouldn't I get to stay?"

Janna laughed. "Good point, Carlie."

"So, it's okay?"

"As long as your parents agree, I see no reason you can't stay until tomorrow," said Janna.

"Okay." Carlie sighed.

"So are we ready to go then?" asked Janna.

Carlie glanced uneasily at the receptionist area now. "Do I need to give them some information or something ..."

"I already gave them your medical form," said Janna. "Now I see why it was important to have that along — like if you had any allergies to medications or anything."

"I meant about the bill and how we pay for it," said Carlie quietly. "I mean, we don't have any insurance, but I know that —"

"Oh, don't worry about that. It's all taken care of already," said Janna.

"Huh?"

"The insurance part I mean."

"Insurance?" Carlie looked curiously at Janna.

"It was part of the ski-trip package. The church insisted on it. No way were we taking a bunch of novice skiers up here without an insurance package. You're totally covered, Carlie."

Carlie smiled. "Cool."

As they drove back to the lodge, Carlie admitted to Janna that she'd been pretty much freaking over the insurance thing. "I thought for sure my parents would be stuck with some humungous bill."

"I wish I'd known you were so worried. I would've told you sooner." Janna turned and smiled at Carlie as she waited for the traffic light to change. "I'm sorry you broke your arm, but I have to admit it's been fun getting to know you better, Carlie. You're a really cool girl."

"Thanks."

"I already know Morgan and Emily pretty well from youth group. They are cool girls too."

"Yeah," agreed Carlie. "They're good friends."

"And I've heard about your club. I think that's great. And it's great that Morgan and Emily encouraged you girls to come on the ski trip. I haven't really gotten to know Chelsea and Amy too well, but they seem nice."

"They're nice ... but they've gotten a little boy crazy lately."

Janna laughed. "That's a funny thing about these trips. A lot of girls your age do get a little boy crazy. Then they go back home and kind of go back to their normal-selves."

"Really?" Carlie felt hopeful.

"Yeah. I've seen it a lot."

Then Carlie told Janna about how Chelsea had been kind of competitive with her. And how she thought it was because Chelsea liked Enrico ... and how Enrico seemed to like Carlie better.

"That makes perfect sense," said Janna.

"And I think Enrico is okay, for a boy anyway, but I don't want him for a boyfriend."

Janna chuckled. "Well, it sounds like you've got a good head on your shoulders, Carlie. I happen to think that all you girls are way too young for boyfriends. In fact, that is exactly what I planned to talk about in cabin time tonight."

"Really?"

"Yep."

"Cool. I hope I get to stay for it."

"Well, get the okay from your parents, and you can."

chapter nine

Morgan and Emily were in the parking lot when Janna and Carlie pulled up. They waved and ran over to meet them.

"How are you?" asked Morgan as she carefully hugged Carlie.

"Better," said Carlie with a real smile.

Then Emily hugged her. "We were praying for you."

"Thanks. It went really well."

"Do you have to go home?" asked Morgan with a frown.

"She's got to call her parents," said Janna as she handed Carlie her cell phone. "If they give her permission, she can stay until tomorrow."

Morgan and Emily cheered, and Carlie cautiously dialed her home number. It was after two, and chances were her mom was home by now. Unless she was at Tia Maria's, and in that case, Carlie would have to try there. But Mom answered on the second ring, and Carlie quickly told her about her little accident, going straight to the insurance situation and how there were no money worries.

"But your arm," said Mom. "Doesn't it hurt a lot?"

"No, it's feeling okay now. I'm fine, really."

"Oh, poor mija. Don't you want to come home?"

"I don't see why," said Carlie. "It's a long trip for you to come up here, and I'll bet the boys are having nap time."

"Not yet, but I was just about to make them."

"So, why don't I just stay here, Mom? Really, I promise you, I'm fine."

"But aren't you in pain?"

"No," said Carlie firmly. And that was mostly true. "The doctor gave me some Advil, and it's really helping. I just want to stay here, Mom. I mean, I paid for the trip, and it's a bummer that I hurt my arm, but it's not really that bad. Can't I please stay and come home tomorrow?"

Now Carlie's little brothers were starting to scream in the background — a sure sign they both needed a nap. "Are you sure?" asked Mom above the noise.

"I'm sure, Mom." Carlie laughed now. "Besides, I'll bet it's a lot quieter up here than at home."

"Yes," she said loudly above the howling. "I'm sure that's true."

"So, I'll be home tomorrow then, okay?"

"Okay," said Mom. "If you're certain, mija. I just don't want you to be in pain or anything."

"The doctor gave me a pill to help me sleep tonight," Carlie told her. "And I'm fine, really, just fine."

So it was settled. Janna talked briefly to Mom too. But when she hung up, it was clear that Carlie was going to stay.

"Yay!" cried Emily and Morgan happily.

"Now," said Carlie, "I'm starving!"

So the three of them went to the café for a late lunch, and then Carlie encouraged her friends to get in some more runs before the lifts closed.

"I can sit by the window and watch," said Carlie. So Morgan and Emily, acting like a couple of mother hens, helped make Carlie comfortable in a big chair in the corner between the picture window and the huge rock fireplace. Then Morgan found a couple of magazines, and Emily brought her a cup of hot cocoa.

"Thanks," said Carlie. "Now you guys go do some snowboarding, okay?"

Morgan shook her head. "No, I'd rather stay here."

"Me too," said Emily.

"Really," insisted Carlie. "You guys need to go have some fun."

"We don't want to leave you."

"Please," begged Carlie. "Can't you see that it's torturous knowing that my good friends are missing out on fun because of me?" Carlie looked at the clock over the fireplace. "You don't even have two hours of riding time left."

"And you'll be okay?" asked Morgan.

"I'm fine."

Of course, Carlie felt mixed emotions after they left. She tried to distract herself with her magazines and cocoa and, really, she was glad that her friends could at least have some fun now. But she did feel lonely too — and left out. She also felt embarrassed for her stupid accident. It was even more humiliating to know that it was partly because of Chelsea that she'd been hurt. Chelsea hadn't exactly dared her. In fact, she'd told her *not* to jump. But she'd done it in a way that had made Carlie feel like she'd be a loser if she didn't. Even before she did it, Carlie had known it was a mistake to jump … and yet she'd gone ahead. She looked down at her injured arm. It was a hard way to learn a tough lesson.

But even more troubling than knowing she'd been stupid was that she felt betrayed by Chelsea now. Betrayed and hurt. Oh, she knew it wasn't really Chelsea's fault that she'd broken her arm. But at the same time she knew she wouldn't have attempted such a daring stunt if Chelsea had kept her big mouth shut.

"Hey, Carlie."

She looked up to see Enrico approaching. His ski hat was in his hands, his hair was all ruffled and sweaty looking, and he had two bright red spots on his cheeks, probably from the cold. But what really got her attention was that he seemed uneasy — like he was almost afraid of her, which was ridiculous.

"Hi, Enrico."

"How are you doing?"

She nodded down to her blue cast and the sling. "Great."

He sat down across from her. "Sorry about that."

She shrugged. "It was my own stupid fault."

"Well, Chelsea kind of egged you on." He shook his head. "I heard her going on about it ... before your run. I could tell that she was kind of challenging you. Then, after you fell, I saw her acting like you were just faking it to get attention. She's such an idiot."

"No, she's just Chelsea. She doesn't always think before she speaks."

"So, you're not mad at her?"

Carlie considered this. "Yeah, I guess I am. But she's in our club ... so I probably shouldn't be mad. I'm pretty sure Morgan would tell me to forgive her. But I guess I don't totally know how to do that."

He nodded. "Me too. I mean, I heard the stuff that Cory said last night about forgiving people, but what if you can't forgive someone? Like what if someone did something so wrong you didn't want to forgive him?"

"I know ... I wondered the same thing."

"So, are you a Christian, Carlie?"

"Yeah, I think I am," she admitted in a way that didn't sound very convincing.

"But you're not sure?"

"No," she said firmly. "I *am* a Christian. I invited Jesus into my heart last summer. But my family, well, we're Catholic, and although we pretty much believe the same things ... I guess I still have some questions. Like I see Morgan and Emily and sometimes it seems like they have something that's different ... like they take their faith really seriously. I guess I kind of want to be like that too."

Enrico studied her closely. "I know what you mean."

"But I'm just not sure what to do about it."

"Cory was telling us some more stuff last night, before we went to bed. Some of the things he said really made me think."

"Like what?"

"Like he said you can pray to God, and he will really hear you. And he'll answer you. Cory makes it sound like God wants to be your best friend ... not just some old dude with a long white beard who lives up in the clouds, you know?"

Carlie nodded. "That's what Morgan and Emily say too."

"But you don't believe it?"

Carlie considered this. "Well, I actually do sort of believe it." Then she told him about some of the things they had prayed about in their club. Like most recently when Emily's family was in trouble, and then the time when she and Chelsea almost drowned. "And it really did seem like our prayers were answered — miraculously."

They talked some more about God and faith and being a Christian, and as they were talking, Carlie almost forgot that Enrico was a boy. It's like their conversation was natural ... and interesting ... it just didn't matter. Then Carlie looked up and noticed that Chelsea, Amy, and Whitney were walking through the lodge now. Chelsea looked in Carlie's direction then quickly turned away as if she was trying to act like she hadn't seen her, although Carlie knew that she had. Still, Carlie wasn't sure why Chelsea would do that. Carlie was also pretty sure that she didn't care. In fact, if she never spoke to Chelsea again, it would be too soon.

Before long, Morgan and Emily showed up. "How's it going?" asked Morgan as she flopped into a chair across from Carlie.

"Good," said Carlie.

Then Jeff came over and joined them, sitting next to Enrico and warming his hands by the fire.

"How was snowboarding?" asked Carlie.

"Pretty good," said Jeff. "The snow was perfect."

"Yeah," said Morgan. "You should've seen my last ride, Carlie. It was awesome."

"She's really getting the hang of it," said Emily.

"Who knows," said Morgan, "by this time tomorrow, I might even try the half-pipe."

"Just make sure you're careful," warned Carlie.

"I'm not going to try to jump," said Morgan quickly.

"Don't let anyone talk you into doing something you don't want to do," said Enrico in a serious tone.

"Well, unless you're a guy," said Jeff. Then he held up his hands when the girls all glared at him. "Just kidding!"

Emily sort of laughed. "Hey, I think we all learned a good lesson today, Carlie."

"Just sorry that it was at your expense," added Enrico.

"And," said Emily, "if it makes you feel any better, Chelsea is feeling a little foolish now. She seemed pretty shocked that your arm was broken."

"Hopefully she's feeling sorry too," said Morgan.

"She should be sorry," said Enrico. "She's partly to blame, you know."

"It's not totally her fault," said Carlie, although to be honest, she still thought Chelsea was sort of responsible. "I mean, it's not like she *made* me do it. It was my dumb choice to jump."

"Even so, Chelsea didn't help much," said Jeff.

The group talked a while longer, and finally the guys noticed what time it was and said they needed to go to their cabin to clean up for dinner.

Carlie blinked in surprise. "You guys actually clean up for dinner?"

Jeff laughed and tugged on the T-shirt beneath his

jacket. "If you smelled me right now you wouldn't even ask that question."

"See ya," called Enrico as they walked away.

Emily chuckled as she poked Carlie in her good arm. "See, even guys have to clean up sometimes."

Carlie looked down at her cast. "Well, even if I wanted to clean up, it would be a challenge now. I don't know how I'm going to take a shower with this thing on. The nurse said not to get it wet."

"We can help you," said Morgan.

"Okay." Carlie slowly stood up then grinned at her friends. "I guess I don't really want to be known as Pigpen after all."

"Not with the way that Enrico was looking at you," said Emily slyly.

"Not because of that," snapped Carlie. "And, besides, we're *just* friends. I am not about to become boy crazy like some other people I won't mention."

"I wasn't saying that you were boy crazy," said Emily.

"Good," said Carlie. "Because I am not."

"Speaking of boy crazy," said Emily, nodding toward the back entrance to the lodge. "There goes Chelsea, Whitney, and Amy right now."

Carlie glanced over in time to see their friends walking toward the game room. All three of them looked like they were on their way to a party or maybe a fashion show, and Carlie could just imagine the smell of perfume floating around them. Well, that was their choice.

"So you're really not mad at Chelsea?" asked Morgan as they went outside into the crisp, cold air.

Carlie took in a deep breath, holding it for a few seconds then slowly letting it go. "I don't know," she admitted. "I guess I'm still sort of mad. I'm trying not to blame her, but she still hurt my feelings when she said I was faking it. I wasn't!"

"Obviously," said Emily.

"And that was wrong of her do that," said Morgan. "She broke the rule of our club." She fumbled with the sleeve of her jacket until she could get the bracelet out, holding it up as a reminder.

"It sure wasn't very loving," said Emily.

"To be honest, I don't feel very much like I love Chelsea right now," said Carlie. The truth was she felt more like she hated the girl. She wished that Chelsea wasn't in their club. It seemed like they had all been a lot happier before Chelsea came along. And yet she knew that was unfair. Not to mention partially her own fault since it had been Carlie who had actually introduced Chelsea to the others in the first place.

"I don't feel very loving toward Chelsea either," admitted Emily.

Morgan sighed. "I hate to say it, but I feel the same

way. I know it's not what Jesus would do either, but I really don't like how Chelsea and Amy are acting all boy crazy and sort of snotty. I'm kind of embarrassed to think that I'm the one who invited them on the ski trip."

"Is there anything we can do about it?" asked Carlie eagerly. She suddenly imagined the three of them standing up to Chelsea and Amy — giving them both a great big piece of their minds and telling them to straighten up or be kicked out of the club. So there!

"I guess we can pray for them," said Morgan.

"That's right," agreed Emily. "We can."

Carlie wanted to shout, "No way!" She wanted to question why they should pray for someone who was acting the way Chelsea had been. And Amy too, for that matter. But instead she just nodded like she agreed. And, right then and there, on the trail halfway between the cabin and the lodge, Emily and Morgan stopped and bowed their heads and prayed. Carlie didn't actually pray, but she pretended to. And when they said "amen" she said "amen" too. But she didn't mean it.

chapter ten

The cabin was hot and stuffy and noisy with girls trying to clean up and get ready for dinner. "Maybe I'll just rest on my bunk for a while," said Carlie as she realized there was a crowd in the bathroom. "Until it thins out in there."

"Good idea," said Morgan. "It's almost an hour until dinner anyway."

Carlie closed her eyes and wished she could fall asleep, but all she could think about was Chelsea now. Despite that nice prayer that Morgan and Emily had prayed, Carlie was feeling more and more anger toward Chelsea. She was replaying everything that Chelsea had said and done since they first came on the ski trip. And each time she replayed it, Chelsea seemed to get worse and worse until Carlie wondered how any of them could possibly stand her. Then Carlie started to remember other things about Chelsea. She remembered how selfish and spoiled Chelsea was, and how she was sometimes snooty because she was richer than everyone else in their club. She even remembered the time Chelsea had shoplifted and not been the least bit sorry for it. Really, Carlie had a whole list of reasons to hate Chelsea. And yet, there were times when they had been friends too. It was confusing. Mostly Carlie knew that Chelsea had hurt her. And for that reason, Carlie decided to keep Chelsea at arm's length — even if it was a broken arm's length.

"Okay," said Emily, gently tapping Carlie on her good shoulder. "It's cleared out in here, time to fix you up."

Carlie sat up and looked around the messy cabin. "Okay …"

"Where's your bag?" asked Morgan.

Carlie pointed to her duffle on the floor at the foot of her bed, and Morgan immediately started to go through it. "How about if you wear your warm-ups?" she suggested, holding up the slightly rumpled Tommy Hilfigers. "That might be easier on your arm."

Carlie nodded. "Yeah, I could probably just sleep in them too."

Emily laughed. "It looks like you already did."

"Hasn't anyone taught you how to pack?" asked Morgan as she continued to rummage through Carlie's bag. "Hey, what's this?" She stood and held out the pink and white polka dot bag.

Carlie rolled her eyes. "My mom must've stuck that in."

"Good for Mom," said Emily as she took the bag and unzipped it. "Yeah, just what you need." Then she paused.

"And there's a note too." She chuckled as she handed the slip of paper to Carlie.

"*Cleanliness is next to godliness,*" read Carlie. "*Love Mom.*"

Morgan and Emily both laughed.

"Is that really in the Bible?" asked Carlie.

"I don't know," said Morgan. "But I do know that God likes to make us clean on the inside."

"And I'm sure he appreciates it when we're clean on the outside too," added Emily. "So, come on, Carlie. It's time to clean up your act."

It was awkward taking a shower with one arm sticking out, but Morgan and Emily did their best to help her and to keep her cast dry. After a while she was clean and dry and dressed in her warm-ups. And, the truth was, it felt pretty good. "I suppose there are better ways to rebel," she admitted, "instead of sacrificing personal hygiene."

"I'll say," said Emily as she fussed with Carlie's curls.

"Hold still," said Morgan, as she put some cherry lip gloss on Carlie's chapped lips.

"There," said Emily finally. "Done."

"And just in time," said Morgan, pointing to the clock.

"Thanks, you guys," said Carlie. "I really do appreciate it."

"So do we!" exclaimed Emily as she helped Carlie with her parka.

"Farewell to Pigpen," added Morgan, and they all laughed.

As they walked back to the lodge, Carlie considered her mom's neat-freak ways. She thought about how hard Mom worked to keep her home and her family clean and fed and well cared for. And then Carlie thought of all the times she'd gotten mad at Mom for those same things. Suddenly she felt bad. Mom was just doing what she thought was best. And even packing that polka dot bag had turned out to be a good thing. Carlie knew that she'd have to thank Mom for that when she got home. And she'd have to apologize too. Just like that, Carlie realized that she had forgiven her mom. And she wasn't mad at her anymore. It seemed slightly miraculous too. Like God had helped her somehow. Then she wondered if the same thing could happen with Chelsea, but she doubted it. That was different!

"How's it going, Carlie?" asked Amy as they sat down at the same table to eat. "Is your arm hurting much?"

"A little," said Carlie, carefully avoiding making eye contact with Chelsea, even though she was sitting directly across from her.

"I miss having you as my buddy," said Whitney.

Carlie looked at Whitney and could tell she was being sincere. "Thanks," said Carlie. "You were a really good buddy — and a good teacher too."

"Well, thank you." Whitney grinned.

"So who was your buddy after I left?" asked Carlie.

"We became a trio," said Amy. "Whitney, Chelsea, and I."

Carlie nodded, still not looking at Chelsea.

"But we stayed off of the half-pipe," said Whitney. "After seeing what happened to you, there was no way I was going to try it."

Amy nodded vigorously. "No way."

"We saw you talking to Enrico," said Whitney in a slightly teasing tone. "Is he your boyfriend now?"

"No," said Carlie sharply. "We're just friends. That's all."

"Sorry," said Whitney, obviously offended.

Carlie softened now. "Sorry," she said quietly. "I didn't mean to bite your head off."

Now the other girls started talking, and as the noise level at their table increased, Carlie was relieved not to be the center of attention anymore. Her friends were sharing various snowboarding stories and almost mishaps and planning for what they would do on the slope tomorrow, and after a while, Carlie started to feel slightly left out. Plus, her arm was starting to ache, and she realized that she'd forgotten to bring her Advil with her.

She reached down to rub her arm, but all she could do was rub the surface of the blue cast. Then, for no rational reason, Carlie wanted to cry. Maybe it had been a mistake to stay here after all. Maybe she should've asked Mom to come get her. If Carlie had been worried about being an outsider before coming up here, she had a lot more cause to feel that way now. The lump in her throat was growing larger. But the last thing she wanted to do was to start bawling in front of her friends.

Then she looked up to see that one other person at their table seemed to be on the outside of things too. Carlie stared at Chelsea across from her. She was just sitting quietly, poking at her barely touched food, her head down, and not talking to anyone. And no one was talking to her either. Just then Carlie felt the tiniest pin prick of pity for Chelsea. It wasn't much ... but it was something. More than that, Carlie felt sorry for herself. But she didn't want to cry.

"Excuse me," she said quietly, although no one seemed to notice. Then she awkwardly got up, and without looking back, she hurried toward the exit. Her plan was to go back to the cabin and get her Advil. Whether or not she came back ... well, she'd figure that out later. Going to bed was actually sounding like a good escape at the moment.

"Hey," said a voice from behind, followed by a hand on her shoulder.

Carlie turned to see Chelsea. "Huh?"

"Where ya going?"

"To the cabin," said Carlie in stiff voice. "My arm hurts, and I forgot my pills."

Chelsea pushed the door open for her. "Mind if I come along?"

Carlie shrugged. "Sure, whatever ..."

They both walked quietly on the trail, snow crunching beneath their boots. Carlie wasn't sure what to say, wasn't sure that she wanted to say anything at all. Finally they were at the cabin, and Chelsea opened the door, waiting for Carlie to go in before she closed it.

Carlie started fumbling through her things, using one hand to check pockets and trying to remember where she'd put the sample packets the nurse had given her.

"Need some help?" offered Chelsea.

"Sure." Then Carlie described the packet and sat down on her bunk to wait for Chelsea to look.

"Here it is," said Chelsea. "Want me to open it for you?"

Carlie nodded.

Then Chelsea went to the bathroom and returned with a glass of water, handing Carlie the pills first and then the glass. Then she sat down beside her on the bunk.

"I'm sorry, Carlie," said Chelsea in a quiet voice.

Carlie blinked. "Really?"

"Yeah. Really."

Carlie wasn't sure what to do now. As mean as it seemed, she wasn't ready for this. She was still mad at Chelsea. And she didn't know if she could let go of that anger. Chelsea didn't deserve it.

"I know you're mad at me," continued Chelsea. "And I guess I can't blame you."

"You can't blame me?" said Carlie bitterly.

"No. I was pretty sure you'd be mad." Chelsea sighed. "But I figured you'd forgive me too."

"Why should I forgive you?" asked Carlie.

Chelsea shrugged.

"How fair is it that you picked on me? Or that you egged me on about jumping on the half-pipe? Or that you made fun of me and called me a liar in front of everyone? How fair is it that you think you can waltz in here and say you're sorry and expect me to forgive you? Just like that. Easy breezy." Carlie stared at Chelsea with narrowed eyes. On one hand, she was shocked by what she was saying, but on the other hand, it felt good to let her feelings out. And, besides, Chelsea deserved this.

"I guess it's not fair ..."

"That's right," snapped Carlie. "It's not. And besides that you go around acting all boy crazy and you make fun of people who aren't and you influence Amy to act like you and you—"

"Fine!" shouted Chelsea as she stood up and faced

Carlie. "You hate me. Go ahead and just say it. You hate me and you'll never forgive me." Tears were streaming down her face now. And then, before Carlie could say a thing, Chelsea turned and ran from the room, slamming the door behind her.

chapter eleven

If Carlie was unhappy before, she was totally miserable now. She considered chasing after Chelsea, but even without a broken arm, it would be hard to catch her. It would be hopeless with her new handicap. Why had Carlie been so mean? What was the point of saying all that? Even if most of it was true, why did she have to say it the way she did? Why couldn't she have been kinder? More like Morgan or Emily? Now Carlie started to cry. More than ever she wanted to go home. She wanted her mom and dad. She wanted her own room. She even wanted her noisy little brothers. But it had been her choice to stay here until tomorrow — she couldn't very well back out now.

"There you are," called out Emily's cheerful voice.

"Is something wrong?" asked Morgan.

Carlie sniffed and went to the bathroom for a tissue.

"What's the matter?" asked Emily when she reemerged.

So Carlie told them about Chelsea, about how she apologized and how she asked Carlie to forgive her ... "And you know what I did?" she sputtered out, "I yelled at her. I told her about everything she'd done that was wrong.

I made her feel really horrible. It was like I wanted to hurt her just as much as she'd hurt me — maybe even more."

"Oh ..." Morgan sat down in a chair and seemed to consider this.

"And what did Chelsea do?" asked Emily.

"She started crying and then took off." Carlie wiped her nose again. "I really hurt her feelings." She sadly shook her head. "And now I feel worse than ever."

"Did you think that you'd feel better if you yelled at her?" asked Emily.

Carlie nodded. "Yeah. Sometimes my mom yells like that. She calls it venting. I hate it when she does it, and I always tell myself that I don't want to be like that ... and then there I go." She sighed. "I'm hopeless."

Emily laughed. "No, you're not."

"It feels like I am."

"Everyone feels hopeless sometimes," said Morgan. "But that's just God's way of reminding us that we need him."

"Well, I guess I really need him."

"Of course you do."

"So ..." Morgan paused as if she was thinking of how to put this. "Well, Carlie, did you even listen to what Cory said last night?"

Carlie shrugged. "Kind of, but it didn't make all that much sense."

"So you didn't get that forgiveness is like a circle?" asked Morgan.

"Not exactly." Carlie looked hopefully at Morgan. "Want to explain it?"

Morgan nodded. "Yeah. To put it simply, Cory said that forgiveness is a circle that shouldn't be broken. Okay?"

"Okay."

"He said that the circle begins with God …" Morgan used her finger to draw a circle in the air. "Up here …" She moved her finger up. "Is where God forgives us." Then she circled down. "And then the circle continues and we forgive others … and that brings us back around to God again. Does that make sense?"

"Kind of."

"But you see, when we circle down here, where we need to forgive others … if we don't, then the circle gets broken and we can't circle back up to God again. It's like we land in a black hole."

"That's where it feels like I am."

"So the way out of that hole is to forgive," said Morgan.

"But how do you forgive someone when you're still angry at them?"

"You ask God to help you," said Emily. Then she told Carlie about how she had to forgive her dad. "I didn't think that it was possible," she admitted. "It just seemed too hard."

Carlie nodded. The story of what Emily's dad had done had been frightening to her. Carlie couldn't even imagine what she would do, or how she would feel if her dad was like that. "Yeah, I can understand that it'd be hard. How did you do it?"

"I had to ask God to help me."

"And did he?"

"Yes. But I realized I had to do my part too. It was kind of like having faith. It's like you take the first step without knowing whether or not the earth is going to give way beneath your feet."

"And did it?"

Emily smiled. "No. And the best part is how good I felt after I forgave my dad."

"What did he do?" asked Carlie.

Emily just shrugged. "I don't know."

"You don't know?"

"No. I just had to forgive him on my own. Then I wrote him a letter and put it in a Christmas card that I took to the jail. I never saw him. And I never heard back from him."

"That was it?"

"The 'it' part of it was that I forgave him, Carlie. With God's help I forgave him. And when I did that, it was like I was suddenly closer to God again. It was like this huge weight was lifted, and I was happy again. How my dad reacted was up to him. I mean, I pray for him, but I can't do anything about his choices."

"So does that make sense?" asked Morgan. She drew a circle with her finger again. "God forgives us, we forgive others, and the circle continues. We refuse to forgive, and the circle is broken."

Carlie nodded now. "Yeah, actually, it does make sense. You guys make a good preaching team."

Morgan and Emily laughed. Then all three of them hugged. And finally, Carlie asked if they could pray for Chelsea again. And this time Carlie prayed too.

"Dear God," she said after the other two finished praying. "I want to forgive Chelsea, but I need your help. I want to be a better friend to her, but I need your help to do that too. Please take care of Chelsea tonight, God, and help me to make things right with her." Then they all said "amen."

"Well, it's time to get back for tonight's meeting," said Morgan. But when they got back to the lodge and went into the meeting room, Carlie looked around and realized that Chelsea wasn't there. As they sang songs, Carlie tried to keep an eye on the door, hoping that Chelsea would walk in. But by the time Cory started his talk, Chelsea was still not there. And now Carlie started to feel worried. She wondered if she should tell Janna. What if Chelsea was lost out in the snow somewhere? And if she was, would it be Carlie's fault? Suddenly, Carlie knew that the only thing to do was to pray. So she bowed her head and without actually saying the words out loud, she began to pray in her head for Chelsea, begging God to keep her safe and bring her back tonight.

Then, just as Carlie lifted her head and opened her eyes, she noticed Chelsea slipping in the door. Her cheeks looked flushed from the cold, and Carlie could tell by the way she slumped into a seat in the back that she was still feeling bad. Carlie knew that was mostly her fault. And she knew she'd have to make things right. Mostly she was just thankful that Chelsea was safe.

"Jesus doesn't expect us to be perfect," Cory was saying now. "He just expects us to give our imperfections to him. He wants us to admit that we blow it, and he wants us to come to him with our failures. But that's not the way our human minds work, is it?" He glanced over the crowd. "Think about how you feel when you mess up. Don't you just want to hide it, sort of bury it and pretend that it never happened? Of course you do. You make a mistake and you don't want to put it on MySpace do you? You don't want everyone to know. But that's not how God works. He tells us to bring our mistakes out into the open. He says to bring our troubles to him. Then he invites us to lay that junk down in front of him, and he asks us to trust him to make things better."

Cory continued on about how God wasn't intimidated by failure, about how God wanted them to live wide-open lives. And as he talked, it began to make more sense. The things that Morgan and Emily had said began to make more sense, and there was a warm sort of electric feeling running through Carlie — like God really was doing something inside of her. And suddenly she was excited about all this. Suddenly she knew that not only was she a Christian — just like Morgan and Emily and the others — but she wanted to be a Christian. She wanted to forgive others, and she wanted to be forgiven. And she wanted so many other things. But first of all, she wanted to settle things with Chelsea.

Then Cory, once again, invited them to give their hearts to God. This time he challenged them to surrender everything. And this time, he asked for anyone who wanted to take their faith to the next level to stand up and come forward. Well, Carlie had never done anything like this before. Certainly not during mass — although they did go forward for communion. But she knew this was different. She knew that she needed to stand up and go forward. Even if she was the only one. So without pausing to question herself, Carlie jumped to her feet and marched forward. To her surprise, several others did too. Then as Cory stood quietly in front, just playing his guitar, more and more kids came forward. Even Jeff and Enrico came forward. And finally Carlie saw that Chelsea had come forward too.

Then Cory prayed with all of them. They all promised to serve God more wholeheartedly than ever. Carlie knew that these weren't just words. She knew that she meant it — all of it.

Then, after Cory said "amen," Carlie went straight to Chelsea. "I'm really, really sorry," she said quickly. "I don't know why I was so mean to you earlier tonight, but I am really, really sorry. And I want you to forgive me. And I totally forgive you. And I want us to be friends and —" But before she could finish, Chelsea was hugging her.

"I'm sorry too, Carlie. I feel really bad about everything. And I know I'm a mean, horrible, selfish person. I was jealous of you, Carlie. And I think I actually wanted you to get hurt, and everything you said about me was true and I don't deserve to — "

"Okay, okay," said Carlie, stepping back. "But don't be so hard on yourself, Chelsea."

"What about what Cory said? What about bringing our messes out into the light?"

Carlie laughed now. "Yes. You're right."

Just then Emily, Morgan, and Amy joined them. All the girls were happily talking about how things were going to be different between them — how important their friendship was and how they wanted to treat each other better. Soon they were all in a group hug, and Carlie was so thankful she hadn't gone home. And she was so thankful for these four girls — and their Rainbow Bus club. She couldn't believe how close they had come to losing it up here on the mountain. But now she thought they'd be closer than ever when they went home.

chapter twelve

Later on they all drifted over to the games room where kids took turns playing pool, ping-pong, or video games. And while Carlie tried to stay involved with her friends, she was getting tired and her arm was starting to ache again. So she sat down with a soda and just watched the buzz of activity all around her.

"Hey," said Whitney as she joined her. "What's up?"

Carlie shrugged. "Not much. I guess I'm kinda tired."

"How's the arm?"

"A little sore."

"That's too bad. Do you wish you'd gone home?"

"No ..." said Carlie slowly. "Not at all. I'm really glad I stayed. Just to be here for Cory's talk tonight was awesome. And then being with my friends ... well, it's worth it."

Whitney nodded. "I saw you and your friends afterward. To be honest, I think I was a little jealous."

"Jealous?"

"Yeah. I mean, I know you and your friends were kind of in a squabble, but it seems like you guys really love each other."

"We do."

"And Amy told me about your club and your clubhouse and everything."

"Did you think it was silly?"

"Not at all. I think it sounds pretty cool. I think you're lucky."

Suddenly Carlie felt uncertain. Was Whitney hinting that she wanted to be involved? But, even if that was the case, it was a decision that would have to be made by the group. Just the same, she knew she would bring it up — when they got back home anyway. But now it was time to go back to the cabins. Janna and Cory were going around and telling kids that it was time to call it a night, and Carlie was glad.

"Janna's going to talk about boys," said Amy with excitement as they walked back to the cabin.

"How do you know?" asked Emily.

"She told me," said Amy.

"She told me too," admitted Carlie.

"This is going to be good," said Amy.

But all Carlie could think about was sleep. She just wanted to crawl into her bunk and close her eyes. And that's just what she did when they got back to the warm cabin. She tried to listen as Janna talked to the girls. Still, she realized it wasn't much different than what Janna had said to her on their way home from the clinic. And it wasn't that much different from what Carlie already believed in her heart. Even though she had learned to appreciate boys, including Enrico, in a new way, she had no interest in anything beyond friendship.

"There will be plenty of time for boyfriends later," Janna was telling the girls. "Right now you should just enjoy being yourself and having good friends. This is a time in your life that can never be repeated, a time when you can grow close to God and learn how to live a life that honors him. Having a boyfriend can really mess that up." Then Janna started telling a story about a thirteen-year-old girl named Jessie who thought the best thing would be to have a serious boyfriend. She hooked up with a guy named Hunter who was sixteen, but it quickly turned into a mess. And, as much as Carlie wanted to hear the end of that story, she was about to drift off to sleep. But she also knew that her friends would retell the story to her tomorrow ... if she asked them to.

Mostly she knew that something really big had changed in her heart tonight. She knew that her commitment to God had deepened, and that her commitment to her friends had deepened as well. And, even with a broken arm and feeling too sleepy to think quite straight, she couldn't wait to see what was going to happen tomorrow. She knew that with God in her life, it would have to be good.

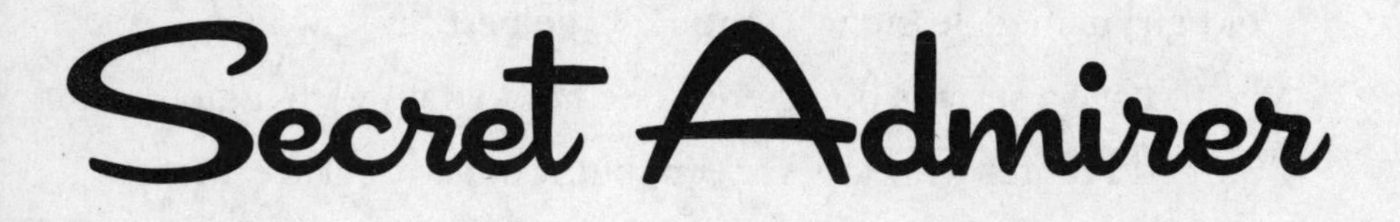
Secret Admirer

chapter one

"So are you guys going to the Valentine's Day dance?" asked Amy.

"Why would we want to do that?" Morgan's brows drew together, and she peered at Amy like she'd just suggested that they all go jump into the ocean. Not a great idea since it was wicked cold and wet outside.

"Yeah," said Carlie, as she picked up a chip and popped it into her mouth. "Who wants to go to some lame dance?"

"Because it'll be fun," said Amy hopefully.

"Fun?" Emily frowned at Amy as she picked up a bead. "You gotta be kidding."

Now Amy regretted bringing the subject up. She looked out at the rain pelting the windows of the clubhouse, a converted school bus. The girls had gathered to spend a rainy Saturday just hanging together, doing beadwork and, of course, eating junk food—well, not *exactly* junk food, but not exactly the kind of food that Amy's mom allowed in her house either.

"What do you plan to *do* at the dance, Amy?" asked Morgan.

"Dance, of course."

"You're actually going to dance with *boys*?" demanded Carlie.

"That's the basic idea." Amy just shook her head as she stared at her three friends. What was wrong with these girls anyway? Why were they so totally clueless when it came to boys?

Emily laughed. "You're nuts, Amy."

"Thanks a lot." Amy frowned. This whole thing about not liking boys did not seem to be improving in the least with her friends. Amy had hoped they'd made some progress on their recent ski trip, but once they got back in school again, everything had gone pretty much back to the same old-same old. Just like always, most of the seventh grade boys would stick to their side of the locker bay with the girls clustered on the other. Not that Amy wanted to be like those girls who were regularly seen globbed onto their boyfriends and sometimes even kissing in front of God and everyone else. But, on the other hand, Amy thought it would be cool to have a guy interested in her. And she knew just which guy she wanted too.

"Seriously, Amy, do you really want to dance with some smelly boy?" asked Morgan.

"Not *all* boys are smelly," argued Amy.

"How many boys have you actually smelled?" teased Emily.

"Which boys *aren't* smelly?" asked Morgan.

"Yeah, are you thinking of some boy in particular?" asked Carlie with a little too much interest. "Anyone we know?"

Amy wished that Chelsea would hurry up and get here. That would help to balance out this discussion. Because Amy knew for a fact that Chelsea planned to go to the dance. In fact, Chelsea probably already had a new outfit all picked out for it — probably something very cool and expensive. And even though Chelsea had given up on Jeff Sanders (since he obviously liked Emily), she hadn't given up on boys in general. In fact, she had already started flirting with that hottie Wade Ketwig. He was an eighth grader and, in Amy's opinion, he was a little out of their league.

But at least Chelsea got it. She understood Amy's desire to go to dances ... to be around boys ... to be liked by boys. Chelsea thought that was just normal. And it was something that she and Amy had in common. Not like Morgan, Carlie, and Emily. They still acted like all boys had cooties, which in Amy's opinion was just so juvenile.

At times like this, Amy found it hard to believe that she was actually the youngest girl in their club. In some ways, she felt she was more mature than most of her friends. Of course, they would never see it that way, and if she even hinted at the possibility, they were quick to remind her of her age. As well as the fact that, although she'd skipped a grade, she was still a whole year younger. They loved to point out that while the rest of them were thirteen (or in Carlie's case, almost thirteen), Amy was still *just twelve*.

So what if they were "teenagers." Really, what was the big deal? It was just a number. But as a result of being younger, they often treated Amy like she was the baby of the group. Sometimes they would tease her or call her a child. Now how ridiculous was that? Not to mention aggravating. Of course, it wasn't much different within her own family. Being the youngest by far of three older siblings, all in their twenties and living in their own house, Amy sometimes felt as if the entire world saw her as *the baby*.

"Hey!" Chelsea greeted them as she burst into the bus. She shook her head, sending droplets of water flying out of her auburn curls. "Did you guys notice that it's raining cats and dogs out there?"

"Any Chihuahuas?" asked Carlie. "I've been begging my mom for one."

"What? So you can carry it around in a purse like Paris Hilton?" teased Amy.

"No," said Carlie quickly. "But I would get a little doggy carryall bag."

"Sorry I'm late," said Chelsea, as she peeled off her soggy Tommy Hilfiger hoody and hung it over the bus's steering wheel to dry. "But my mom just had to stop by the bakery on the way over here. And it took her like forever to order some stupid cake for the dinner party they're having tonight."

"What kind of cake?" asked Amy.

"Something dark chocolate with no flour.Sounded pretty weird, if you ask me." Chelsea looked around the bus. "So, what's up?"

"Amy's freaking over the Valentine's Day dance," said Morgan.

"Huh?" Chelsea peered at Amy.

"I'm so relieved you're here," said Amy. "I simply asked if anyone was going to the Valentine's Day dance, and they all acted like I'd totally lost my mind."

"Is that all?" Chelsea slid into the seat by the table, across from Amy. "Of course we're all going to the dance," she announced with confidence.

"Says who?" challenged Morgan. She adjusted her glasses then carefully strung a bright blue glass bead over the needle and onto the growing strand of colorful beads.

"Says Honor Society," declared Chelsea.

"Huh?" Emily looked confused. "What do you mean?"

"Well, as you guys know, we all made good enough grades to make the honor roll," pointed out Chelsea.

"Barely," said Carlie.

"You and me both," admitted Chelsea. "But the point is that we made the first cut."

"First cut?" Morgan frowned. "What's that supposed to mean?"

"It means that making the honor roll is the first step, but if we want to make it into Honor Society, we have to continue keeping our grades up, and besides that we need to show some genuine interest."

"What kind of genuine interest?" asked Emily.

"And what can that possibly have to do with the Valentine's Day dance?" asked Carlie.

"I get it," said Amy suddenly. "Honor Society sponsors the Valentine's Day dance, right?"

"Exacto-mundo," said Chelsea as she took a chip and dipped it into the salsa then popped it into her mouth. "Umm, this is good. Homemade?"

"My mom," said Carlie.

"She should sell this."

Carlie shrugged.

"Back to the dance," said Amy with even more impatience.

"Right," said Chelsea. "So Vanessa Price, she's an eighth grader — you know who I mean?"

"We know," said Morgan in a slightly bored tone.

"*Everyone* knows who Vanessa is," said Carlie.

"Vanessa Price, the most popular girl in eighth grade," said Emily as if reciting the words. "Cheerleader, president of Student Council, editor of the newspaper, pretty brunette with perfectly straight teeth."

"And she's nice," added Amy.

"Yes," said Chelsea. "She actually is nice. And she told me that if we want to make it into Honor Society, it would help if we volunteered for the Valentine's Day dance."

"You mean they want us to volunteer to dance?" said Morgan. "I can do that." Then she got up and started to do some dance step that Amy had never seen before, but had to admit was impressive.

"I call it the Electric Porcupine," said Morgan.

They all clapped, and she bowed then sat back down and returned to her beading.

"Where did you learn that?" asked Emily.

"I made it up."

"I learned a fun dance from *High School Musical*," said Chelsea.

"Can you teach us?" asked Morgan.

"Wait a minute — wait a minute." Amy banged her fist on the table so hard that the bowl of chips jumped. "First things first — we need to finish discussing the Valentine's Day dance."

"What's to discuss?" asked Carlie.

"Well, like Chelsea said," persisted Amy, "if it will increase our chances of making it into Honor Society, we should participate, don't you think?"

"I think you don't need any help getting into Honor Society," pointed out Carlie. "You always make straight A's, Amy."

Amy nodded, trying not to appear too smug. This was true. Her grade point average was always perfect. She would settle for nothing less. "But what about you, Carlie? And you, Chelsea?"

"My point exactly," said Chelsea.

"But what's the big deal about being in Honor Society anyway?" asked Morgan. "I mean, who really cares?"

"Who cares?" asked Amy. She was stunned. "How can you *not* care?"

Morgan shrugged and reached for another bead.

"I actually do care," admitted Emily. "I plan to keep my grades up throughout high school. I hope to get an academic scholarship. I want to go to a good journalism school."

"And my dad hopes that I'll be the first one in his family to go to college," said Carlie.

"And that's all just fine," said Chelsea. "But I'm talking about the present, the here and now. I'm talking about the Honor Society perks."

"Perks?" inquired Amy.

"Yeah," said Chelsea. "Vanessa told me they have this really great overnight, all-expenses-paid trip every spring where they go someplace really fun. Last year they went to Portland where, besides other things, they went ice-skating and to the theater and stayed in a really swanky downtown hotel — and they got to miss two full days of school too."

"Cool," said Carlie.

"So," continued Chelsea. "We all need to volunteer to help with the Valentine's Day dance to make some Brownie points."

Amy nodded. "And if we help with the dance, it seems only appropriate that we should attend the same dance."

"Right," agreed Chelsea. "Of course."

Amy grinned. She'd known that Chelsea would support her on this. Chelsea got it.

"So what will we volunteer to do for the dance?" asked Carlie. She held up her arm, still in a cast from her snowboarding mishap. "I get this removed next week, so I should be able to do something."

"Decorations," proclaimed Chelsea. "Vanessa said that no one ever wants to do decorations. And she is heading up the committee and suggested that I should volunteer."

"Why does no one like to do decorations?" asked Carlie. "I think it sounds kinda fun."

"She said it's because you have to do all the decorating right before the dance, and that last hour is crazy because you have to get everything up in the cafeteria, and it's a zoo. Vanessa said you end up all sweaty and messy. Apparently none of the eighth grade girls ever want to do it, so it's kind of an initiation to get the seventh graders to help out."

Amy frowned now. "So we have to go to the dance all sweaty and messy?"

"Talk about those smelly boys," teased Carlie. "Wait until they get a whiff of us."

"I have a plan," said Chelsea. "We'll just bring our dressy clothes and shoes and stuff in bags. And then, after we're done decorating, we'll do a quick clean up and be all ready for the big dance."

"Perfect," said Amy. She smiled hopefully at her friends.

"So, are you guys all in to help decorate?" asked Chelsea.

"I am," said Emily.

"Okay," agreed Morgan.

"I guess so," added Carlie. "Although I'm not so sure I can keep my grades high enough to stay on the honor roll, so it might be a waste of time for me."

"Why's that?" asked Morgan.

Carlie looked a little embarrassed. "I'm having a hard time in Algebra One right now. I just don't get it."

"I can help you," offered Amy. Math just happened to be one of her best subjects, and she was actually taking Algebra *Two* this year, the only seventh grader in the class. Not that she needed to brag. Everyone was pretty much aware of her academic skills.

Carlie brightened. "Hey, that'd be great."

"And, speaking of grades, I'm kind of floundering in Spanish just now," admitted Chelsea. "It's like I'm language impaired or something."

"Hey, I can help with that," said Carlie proudly.

"Would you?" asked Chelsea eagerly.

"Sí, amiga. No problema." Carlie laughed.

"I have an idea," said Morgan suddenly. "Why don't we have at least one homework meeting each week — you know, where we help each other with various subjects. I mean, it's like we all have these different strengths and stuff."

"Like Emily is a fantastic writer," said Chelsea.

"And Morgan is Mr. Hilliard's favorite in social studies class," pointed out Emily. "She always knows everything about everything in there."

"So we can schedule a weekly time to meet here and help each other out," continued Morgan with enthusiasm. "That way we'll all keep our grades up and we can all stay on the honor — "

"Great idea," said Amy, "But before we get all distracted, I want to take a vote."

"A vote for what?" asked Emily.

"For the dance," said Amy impatiently.

"I thought we already agreed," said Chelsea.

"We agreed to decorate," explained Amy. "But I want us to agree that we'll all go to the dance."

Morgan rolled her eyes and groaned. "What if we don't *want* to dance?"

"But you like to dance," protested Amy. "We just saw you."

"But that's different," said Morgan. "It's just you guys."

"Is it because of your church?" asked Chelsea suddenly.

"I mean, I had this friend back in California, and her church said that it was a sin to dance."

"A sin to dance?" Morgan looked shocked. "No, of course it's not a sin to dance — at least not in my church anyway. Sometimes we even dance during worship service."

"You dance at church?" Amy tried not to look too shocked.

"Well, not like couples dance," Morgan told her. "I mean, we dance as a form of worship. Like you're so happy to be singing to God that you can't keep your feet from moving too."

"Yeah," said Emily. "It's really fun."

"Dancing at a dance is fun too," said Chelsea.

"Anyway, let's get this nailed down, okay?" Amy held up a hand. "I motion that we take a vote, President Morgan."

"I second the motion," said Chelsea.

"Fine," said Morgan with a lack of enthusiasm. "Who is in favor of attending the Valentine's Day dance?"

To Amy's relief, they all raised their hands. To be honest, other than Chelsea, the others still seemed fairly reluctant, but at least it was agreed upon now. They had given their word, and they would all go to the dance. Amy couldn't wait!

chapter two

On Sunday afternoon, Amy began to make a plan. She would spend the upcoming week doing whatever she could to catch a certain guy's eye. Her goal was to make him like her before the big dance. Okay, she knew she couldn't actually *make* him like her. But perhaps she could at least make some kind of connection. Because, more than anything, Amy wanted Brett Woods to invite her onto the dance floor at the Valentine's Day dance. Nothing would make her happier than for her friends to stand on the sidelines with their mouths hanging open as she and Brett actually danced. Now the big question was — what could she do to get Brett to notice her?

Amy stood in front of the mirror and frowned as she studied her image. It wasn't easy being small for her age. Some people even assumed she was still in grade school. Just last week, a teacher's aide had asked if she was in the wrong school or needed directions. Amy looked at the outfit she had worn to church that morning. It was pretty much her typical wardrobe, but it did nothing to make her look older. Even her sleek black hair, cut in a bob which was now reaching to her shoulders, looked sort of juvenile. Somehow she had to change her image.

As a result, a couple of hours later, Amy's previously orderly room looked like her closet had exploded. A variety of shirts, pants, skirts, jeans, and shoes were splayed all over her bed, dresser, and floor. She'd already tried on about a hundred outfits, but everything she owned seemed totally childish — like things a grade school girl would wear. She wanted to look older, more sophisticated. But how?

She considered calling Chelsea, but she knew that Chelsea and her mom had driven up the coast to go to the outlet mall to do some shopping and probably weren't even home yet. Why couldn't Amy have a mom like Chelsea's? Amy's mom was hopelessly old-fashioned, could care less about style, and thought that fashion was a big waste of money. Her mother had worn the exact same clothes for years. In fact, Amy couldn't remember her mother ever buying anything new. Not even shoes. "These are good for work," her mother would protest when her daughters gave her a bad time about her boring selection of ugly white athletic shoes.

Seriously, Amy sometimes felt that the only thing her mother ever thought about was the restaurant. Although, to be fair, Amy also knew that it was only because of her mother's fierce work ethic that the family business managed to support them all like it did. And Amy knew she should be thankful. Still, she sometimes secretly wished there was no such thing as Asian Garden.

Finally, feeling completely hopeless, she dialed An's cell phone number. An was, in Amy's opinion, *the good sister*. Not only was she much kinder than her oldest sister Ly, she had a good sense of style as well.

"Hey, Amy," said An cheerfully. "What's up?"

"I need some fashion help," moaned Amy.

An laughed, but not in a mean way. "What kind of help are you looking for?"

So Amy explained her problem. "All my clothes are so babyish, An. And all my friends are older than me. And I hate looking like the baby all the time."

"Uh-huh ..."

Amy could hear the background noise at the restaurant, and she knew An was probably busy, but she also knew that she was desperate. "I really, really need your help, An," she begged.

"So, what can we do?" asked An. "I mean, you know that the restaurant doesn't close until nine, and there's no place to shop around here at that time of night."

"I know ..." Amy let out a sad little sigh.

"How about tomorrow?" said An brightly. "I could pick you up after school, and we could do a little shopping together. Would you like that?"

"That'd be fantastic!" Then Amy thanked her and

hung up. Okay, that didn't exactly solve tomorrow's outfit, but Amy decided she'd just have to make do for the time being.

On Monday morning, Amy walked to school with Carlie, Morgan, and Emily. They were chattering away, just like usual, but all Amy could think about was Brett Woods. She knew it was kind of silly, and she knew her friends would probably tease her if they knew, but she just couldn't help herself. With his sandy blond hair and expressive brown eyes, Brett was by far the cutest guy in seventh grade. Also, he was smart and athletic. And, although Amy suspected that lots of girls had crushes on him, he did not have a girlfriend. Yet.

Amy had two classes with Brett — English and social studies — and she daydreamed about him more than she would ever admit. Her favorite daydream, the one she was having as they walked to school, was the one where they were at the dance together. She was wearing a pretty print skirt and embroidered top that she'd seen in one of Chelsea's fashion magazines. And Brett had on a neat white shirt and chinos. In her fantasy, he shyly approached her, asked her to dance and, while her friends were gawking, he took her by the hand and led her to the center of the dance floor where they danced, not just one dance, but until the last song of the dance.

"Earth to Amy," said Morgan in a loud voice.

"What?" Amy turned to see that all three friends were staring at her.

"What's up with you?" asked Emily.

"Yeah," said Carlie. "It's like you're on another planet."

"Sorry," said Amy quickly. "Just thinking about something."

"Probably a boy," teased Carlie.

"No," said Amy. "I was thinking, uh, about an assignment in English."

"Yeah, right," said Morgan in a tone that sounded skeptical.

"Anyway," said Emily. "We were asking you which day works for our homework meeting. We all thought Tuesday was good. But we know you sometimes work at the restaurant."

"Tuesday is fine,"said Amy. "I can arrange to have it off."

"Great," said Carlie. "Now tell us which boy you were daydreaming about."

Amy felt her cheeks getting warm.

"See," teased Carlie. "I knew it was a boy."

"None of your business," said Amy as she shifted her clarinet case to the other hand. She started walking faster. "And if you guys don't hurry, I'm going to be late for band."

"How can you possibly be late?" asked Carlie, glancing at her watch.

"Late for Amy means not being early," Morgan reminded her friends.

"And I *need* to be early," Amy told them. She had switched from orchestra to band this year, and so far she had only made second chair in clarinet.

"Are you still worried about being the best clarinet player?" asked Emily.

"It's only natural," said Amy, happy to have distracted her friends away from the daydreaming stuff. "I was always first chair flute before I switched instruments."

"So who is first chair clarinet?" asked Carlie.

"That geeky Oliver Fitzgerald," she told them.

"That's not very nice," pointed out Morgan.

"Sorry," said Amy. "Okay, he's not really a geek. But he sure dresses like one. He even has a pocket protector."

"Isn't he an eighth grader?" asked Emily.

"Yes." Amy nodded. "And he's a Mr. Know-It-All when it comes to band. It's like he thinks I'm a total idiot, because he's always telling me what to do and how to do it."

"And you'd probably like to tell him what to do instead, *Miss Ngo It All*," teased Morgan. And they all laughed. Even Amy. It had been a while since anyone had used her old nickname. And it was a good reminder to her that she should probably watch what she said about others — particularly that obnoxious Oliver Fitzgerald. Or, as An would say, "people in glass houses shouldn't throw rocks." Still, it would be easier if Oliver didn't provide such a big target. And, if Amy didn't have him in two classes — band and Algebra Two.

"Anyway," said Morgan. "Monday was our second choice for homework night. So if Chelsea has a problem, maybe we'll have it this afternoon."

"I can't," said Amy. "I'm going shopping with An."

"Shopping for what?" asked Emily.

"Just stuff." Amy wasn't sure she wanted to go into details just yet.

"Probably something for the dance," said Morgan in a suspicious tone.

"Maybe," said Amy. "Or maybe I just want to change my image."

"Why?" asked Carlie. "I think your image is fine."

Amy frowned now. "I look way too young."

"Too young for what?" asked Morgan.

Amy stopped walking now and stared at her three friends. "Look at you guys," she said, pointing to them. "You all look so much older than me. It's just not fair."

Morgan laughed. "Well, we are older, Amy."

"And you're petite," said Carlie.

"And we happen to think you're cute just the way you are," added Emily. "You don't need to change anything."

"Well, I want to," declared Amy. "And An has agreed to help. So today is definitely not going to work for me. Okay?"

Carlie suddenly held up her cast. "I just remembered — it won't work for me either. I get this thing off today, right after school."

"I'll bet you can't wait," said Emily.

"Totally," said Carlie.

They arrived at school, and the girls soon parted ways. Amy hurried toward the locker bay to unload some things from her overloaded backpack. But just as she reached her locker, she noticed that Brett was standing right next to it. Was it possible that he was looking for her? But as she got there, he simply turned and walked away — as if he hadn't even seen her. She tried not to feel too disappointed as she opened her locker. As usual, her locker was neat and orderly, but there was a piece of folded notebook paper with her name printed neatly on one of the folded sides. It seemed that someone had slipped a note into her locker for her. How odd. Amy peered down the locker bay just in time to see Brett ducking around the corner. Was this note possibly from him?

Of course, she knew that was a totally ridiculous idea — and probably just the result of too many Brett Woods daydreams, but as she opened the note, she was suddenly not so sure.

Dear Amy Ngo,

You are the prettiest and smartest girl in the entire school, and I really, really like you. Someday I will reveal my true identity. Until then I will remain Your Secret Admirer (YSA).

♥ YSA

Amy blinked in disbelief as she read the note again — more slowly this time. The penmanship was neat and blockish, and the spelling was correct. Had Brett Woods possibly slipped this into her locker? Her heart pounded with excitement as she quickly rearranged her backpack, closed her locker, and hurried toward the music department. The note was safely tucked into a pocket of her backpack, and she planned to read it more carefully later. Somehow she had to find out who YSA really was — and whether or not it was Brett Woods. She couldn't wait to tell Chelsea! In fact, she would call her right now.

"I'm on my way to band," she said breathlessly, "but I can't wait to talk to you, Chelsea. Something totally amazing has happened."

"What?" demanded Chelsea.

"No time to tell you now," said Amy as she went into the band room. "But I'll show you at lunch, okay?"

"Okay, but now I'm going to be dying of curiosity."

"Later," said Amy, hanging up and turning off her phone. Cell phones were a controversial topic at their school. They were close to being outlawed altogether, and you could get into real trouble just for having one on during class. But Amy was always careful with hers.

"Hey, Number Two," said Oliver as Amy took her seat in the band room. "What's up?"

"My name is Amy," she told him for the umpteenth time.

"You'll always be Number Two to me," he teased.

"Always?" She felt her brows arch in that expression that her friends had warned her could come across as snotty or superior if she wasn't careful. But it felt like she couldn't help it with this guy. Why did Oliver Fitzgerald insist on being so obnoxious?

He laughed. "Do you seriously think you can unseat me, Number Two?"

"I can seriously try," she said as she snapped open her clarinet case.

"Bring it on," he told her. Then he continued warming up, perfectly too. Naturally, this only served to remind Amy that winning first chair was going to continue to be an uphill battle. Still, Amy wasn't about to give up. Besides, she was in an extra good mood today. Without even trying, it seemed that she had caught Brett's eye. Because the more she thought about it, the more certain she felt that she had nearly caught him in the act. Surely he had to be YSA! The big question now was what should she do about it? Obviously, he was too shy to say anything just yet. Maybe, like her, he had been daydreaming about them getting to know each other. Maybe this was his way of making the first step. She couldn't wait to see what might happen next. But for now, she knew she better stay focused on her music.

chapter three

"Wow," said Chelsea as she reread the note. "You're certain that this is from Brett Woods."

"Not absolutely," admitted Amy. "But I did see him right next to my locker … and then the note was there." They were standing in the lunch line now. Morgan, Emily, and Carlie were already heading for their regular table.

"Are you going to tell them?" asked Chelsea as she nodded toward the others.

"I don't know …" Amy frowned. "I'm sure they'll tease me."

"Or be impressed," said Chelsea. "I mean, everyone knows that Brett Woods is one of the coolest guys in seventh grade."

"I know," said Amy happily. "I can't believe this is happening."

"Hey, there he is," said Chelsea, nodding over toward the main door. "Maybe you should wave."

"No way," said Amy. She felt her cheeks flushing now, and she looked the other direction.

"Want me to talk to him?" offered Chelsea.

"No," said Amy quickly. "I want to wait and see what he does next."

"When's your next class with him?"

"Not until seventh. It's English."

"Maybe he'll offer to walk you home," said Chelsea.

"Oh, I don't think so ..." And suddenly Amy wasn't sure how she'd feel about that. It was one thing to daydream about Brett ... and the dance and all ... but the idea of him actually walking her home was kind of weird.

They had barely sat down at the table with their friends when Chelsea blurted out Amy's big news.

"Seriously?" said Emily.

Amy nodded.

"Can we see it?" asked Morgan.

"I don't want to get the note out right now," said Amy, glancing over to where the cool seventh grade boys were sitting. "He might see me and feel uncomfortable."

"You really think it's from Brett?" asked Carlie.

"He was the only one by my locker," said Amy. "And then I found the note."

"But someone could've put it in earlier," suggested Morgan. "Someone that you didn't see."

"I just have a very strong feeling it was Brett," said Amy stubbornly.

"And he was looking our way when he came into the cafeteria," pointed out Chelsea. "I saw him."

"But writing a note?" questioned Emily. "He doesn't really seem like the type."

"How do you know?" demanded Amy.

"Just a hunch."

"Well, sometimes hunches are wrong." Amy opened one end of her straw and blew the wrapper off, directly into Emily's nose. "And now, let's talk about something else, okay?" She turned to Chelsea. "How was the outlet mall?"

Fortunately, Chelsea distracted everyone with a detailed description of a "fabulous" outfit that she'd gotten for the Valentine's Day dance. And as Chelsea rambled on, Amy sneaked peeks at Brett. And it seemed like he was looking directly at her too. This was just too perfect! She could not wait until English!

But seventh period came and went, and Brett never said boo to her.

"I'm so bummed," she admitted to Chelsea. It was starting to rain again, and they were seeking shelter under the overhang by the front door, keeping an eye out for their rides. An was picking up Amy and, as usual, Chelsea's mom was playing chauffeur for her.

"Why don't you let me talk to him for you?" said Chelsea eagerly.

"I don't know ..." Amy sighed. "I don't want to push things too fast. I mean, he's obviously shy. I should just let him handle this his way. Don't you think?"

"I don't know." Chelsea shook her head. "Sometimes

guys need a little boost, you know. A little encouragement. I wouldn't have to mention the note, Amy. I could just hint that you might like him."

"Let me think about it," said Amy. She spotted An's little car coming their way and waved. "I'll get back to you on it, okay?"

"Okay. Have fun shopping."

"I wish you could come," said Amy.

"Me too, but there's no getting out of the orthodontist. I just hope he doesn't decide to put me back in braces." She made a face. "Wouldn't that be perfect for the Valentine's Day dance."

"Good luck," called Amy as she ran toward An's car.

"Ready to rock and roll?" asked An as Amy hopped in.

Amy grinned and nodded. "You won't believe what happened to me today," she told her sister as she pulled back onto the street.

"Did you make first chair?"

"Better than that," said Amy. Then she told her the whole story, even reading the note, which she had actually memorized now.

"Wow, pretty exciting stuff," said An as she got onto the highway.

"It's like my dreams are coming true," said Amy happily.

"So, what will you do if the note really is from Brett?" asked An.

"Besides being deliriously happy?"

"Yes. I mean, will you guys become boyfriend/girlfriend?"

Amy shrugged. "Oh, I don't know ..."

"No offense, but you seem kind of young for that sort of thing, Amy."

Amy frowned at her sister. "I thought you'd understand."

"It's not that I don't understand, Amy. But getting serious about a boy in middle school ... well, it just seems too much ... too soon."

"What do you mean by *serious?*" asked Amy.

"You know, like you're going out, or going steady or dating, whatever you call it."

"Going out."

"Right." An nodded. "Would it be like that?"

"I don't know," admitted Amy.

An smiled. "Yes, I'm probably making this into a big deal. Sorry. But I just happen to care about my baby sister."

"I'm not a baby."

"That's right. I know you're not. I can't believe how quickly you're growing up too, Amy. So, let's talk about clothes. What do you have in mind?"

Naturally, Amy didn't even know what she had in mind. But, as it turned out, An was full of good ideas. And Amy went to some of the same outlet mall stores that

Chelsea had told her about. By the time they finished, Amy had spent most of her tip money, saved up during the holidays when they'd been unusually busy, and accumulated a number of "older-looking" items of clothing as well as a very cool outfit for the upcoming dance. She couldn't have been happier. Well, almost anyway.

"How about makeup?" asked Amy as she paused in front of a cosmetics store.

"Oh, I don't know about that, Amy."

"Why not?"

"Well, for one thing there's Mom. For another thing there's Dad."

"But you and Ly use makeup," protested Amy.

An laughed. "Yes, and we're a whole lot older than you, Amy." An frowned. "I'm already freaking over the shoes you got. Mom will have a fit when she sees them."

"But they make me so much taller," Amy pointed out.

"But you could fall and break an ankle if you're not careful."

"Other girls at school wear them. I've never seen anyone trip."

"You're not *other* girls, Amy. And Mom will make that crystal clear when she sees those shoes."

"Maybe Mom won't see my shoes."

"Oh, Amy," said An as she attempted to tug Amy away from the front of the cosmetics store. "I know you want to be grown-up now, but trust me, it'll all come soon enough."

But Amy wasn't budging. "How old were you when you started wearing makeup, An?"

"Sixteen. Well, officially that is. To be honest I was sneaking it before that — but I was still around fifteen I think."

"Really?" Amy frowned. Fifteen seemed a long way off.

"And just so you know Ly was *eighteen*."

"No way! That's old enough to vote."

"You know how old-fashioned our parents are. Dad honestly used to believe that only *disrespectable* women wore makeup."

"But not now?"

"He's come a long way. And so has Mom. But, trust me, Amy, they will both say that twelve is way too young for makeup."

"You mean besides lip gloss." With An's help, Amy had somehow slipped lip gloss beneath the parental radar screen.

"Yes. Besides lip gloss."

"I sometimes use Chelsea's makeup," Amy admitted as she looked longingly in the store window. "Her parents think *she's* old enough."

"Well, ours do not, Amy. And if they catch you wearing makeup, you can count on fireworks."

"Couldn't you just sort of look away?" asked Amy as she peered into the store window. "I mean, if I sort of sneaked in and got a couple of things?"

An frowned. "Well, I obviously can't keep you from buying makeup if you're that determined. I mean, there are plenty of places in town, and you have your own money. All I can do is warn you, little sister."

"I just need to look older," pleaded Amy. "I want Brett to really notice me — I want him to take me seriously."

"But what about that note?" asked An suddenly. "Didn't he already think you were pretty?"

Amy considered this. "Yes ..."

"And you *are* pretty, Amy." An peered down at her. "You have a beautiful complexion and nice dark lashes. You don't need makeup. Why not leave well enough alone?"

"I want to look older, An."

An held up her hands in a helpless gesture. "It's your life, Amy. Just don't tell Mom and Dad that I encouraged you."

"Well, you didn't."

"And for that matter, don't tell Ly either. She's so grumpy lately."

"And why is that exactly?" asked Amy. "Is she still jealous of you?"

"She thinks she needs a boyfriend," said An sadly. "But I think she needs God. And whenever we talk, it usually ends up in an argument."

"I better not tell her that I might have a boyfriend," said Amy.

"That's for sure. Ly would probably throw something at you."

"Poor Ly." Amy peered longingly in the cosmetic-store window again.

"Yes. If anyone could use a secret admirer just now, it is our older sister." An sighed.

"I'm going in there," said Amy quickly.

"You're sure you want to do this?"

"I am," said Amy, acting more confidently than she felt. And, of course, she was barely inside the door when she realized she was in way over her head when it came to cosmetics.

It was one thing to borrow items from Chelsea — like she'd done on the ski trip — but trying to figure this out on her own? That seemed hopeless. She was just about to make a quick exit when the woman at the counter asked to help her.

"I don't know much about makeup," Amy said cautiously. "But I'm in middle school, and all my friends look older than me and I — "

"I'm sure we have just what you need," said the

woman. And before long, Amy was not only buying blush, she also had eyeliner, eye shadow, mascara, and a sweet little daisy-print bag to keep them in.

"Oh, dear," said An when Amy finally emerged.

"I know the woman probably put too much makeup on me," admitted Amy. "But I'll wipe it off before Mom and Dad see me."

"You better." An just shook her head.

Amy used tissues to remove the makeup as An drove them home. Monday was the only day that the restaurant was closed, and Amy could count on the fact that at least one of her parents would be home when she got there.

"How was shopping?" asked Mom as Amy came into the house.

"Great," she said.

Mom scowled. "I don't see why you needed new things, Amy. You have lots of nice clothes."

"*Everyone* looks older than me, Mom. All my friends — "

"All your friends *are* older than you, Amy. You know that."

"But I don't like being different."

Mom threw up her hands. "Everyone is different."

"Well, I used my own money," Amy pointed out.

"You mean you *wasted* your own money." Then her mom began to go on about how they used to be so poor and how they never had money for fancy clothes and how Amy should be thankful...

"Yes, yes," said Amy as she made her way to her bedroom. "I am thankful, Mom. Very, very thankful."

Her mom continued rambling now, reverting to her native Vietnamese tongue, and Amy knew that she hadn't heard the end of the lecture against wasteful spending. Still, she felt it was worth it as she tried on some of her outfits, complete with makeup. Because suddenly, she did look older. And maybe Brett had already noticed her — but now he would notice her even more. How could he not? And maybe he would feel brave enough to actually speak to her now.

chapter four

"Whoa!" exclaimed Morgan as Amy joined her three friends in Morgan's carport on Tuesday morning. Morgan's grandmother was driving them to school since it was, once again, pouring down rain.

"What happened to you, Amy?" asked Emily.

Amy just shrugged, glancing over her shoulder and wishing her friends would just chill. "Nothing ..."

"You're wearing makeup!" said Carlie with a shocked expression.

"So?" Amy turned and looked directly at her friends. "No big deal."

"And look at your shoes," said Morgan. "You're almost as tall as Emily now."

"Aren't you worried you might break an ankle in those things?" asked Carlie as she held up her arm, finally cast-free, as if to make her point.

"No, I'm not," said Amy. She glanced at her watch now. "So, Morgan, is your grandma taking us to school or not?"

"Here I am, girls," said Morgan's grandmother as she

emerged from the house jingling her car keys. "Let's get this show on the road."

"How are you feeling, Mrs. Evans?" Amy asked. Okay, so this was a partial attempt to distract her friends from her new look, but she had been concerned about the old woman's health. They all had.

Morgan's grandmother smiled. "Pretty good, Amy, all things considered. But it does feel good to get out a bit. Being stuck in the house for weeks wasn't much fun. Thank you for asking."

"Grandma's only been driving for a week now," said Morgan. "So we'll have to keep an eye out for her and make sure she doesn't run any red lights or anything." Morgan grinned at her grandma.

"Don't you girls worry about me," said Mrs. Evans. "I've been driving for more than fifty years now. A couple of months of prescribed rest haven't affected my driving skills in the least."

They all piled into the car, and Amy turned her face away from her friends, pretending to look out the window and hoping they'd forget about her change in appearance. To be honest, Amy was having second thoughts herself. She wondered if it was really worth all the trouble to try to look older. For starters, it hadn't been easy sneaking past her mom this morning. She had eaten breakfast first then sneaked back to the bathroom where she'd quickly applied makeup before she grabbed up her backpack and slipped on her new shoes. Then she'd hollered a quick good-bye and dashed out the door and over to Morgan's. But then she'd almost tripped in her shoes. And that was after practicing walking in them for nearly an hour last night. Looking older was proving to be a real challenge.

"Seriously, Amy?" asked Carlie from the other side of the backseat. "What's up with the makeup anyway?"

"Nothing is up," said Amy. "I'm just trying something new."

"You mean you're just trying to catch a boy," teased Morgan from the front seat.

"Morgan Natalia," scolded her grandmother. "It's not nice to tease little Amy."

"It's true," said Morgan. "She is trying to catch a boy — aren't you, Amy?"

Amy folded her arms across her front and pressed her lips together.

"Well, Amy wouldn't need to use makeup to catch a boy," said Grandma. "She's already a very pretty girl just as she is."

So then Emily had to go and tell Morgan's grandmother all about Amy's secret admirer and the note. Amy suddenly wished she hadn't told anyone. Why hadn't she kept her secret admirer a secret?

"Oh my," said Mrs. Evans. "How exciting to have a

secret admirer, Amy. I remember once, a long time ago, when I had someone like that." She sighed. "It was such fun trying to figure out who that admirer was."

"Who was it?" asked Morgan.

Her grandmother laughed. "It turned out to be your grandfather's very best friend Henry Lake."

"What did my grandfather think of that?" asked Morgan indignantly. "Did he punch this Henry right in the nose?"

Mrs. Evans laughed even louder now. "No, not at all ... your grandfather and I weren't even going together way back then. But Henry got your grandfather's attention, and before long your grandfather became my not-so-secret admirer, and within a year we were happily married."

"How romantic," said Amy.

Carlie giggled. "So, do you think Brett Woods is going to propose to you today, Amy?"

Amy rolled her eyes. A statement that stupid did not deserve a civilized response.

"Well, you girls have a good day," called Mrs. Evans as they piled out of the car, running through the rain up the front steps. Amy had to be careful not to stumble in her new shoes.

"Amy," said Emily once they were all inside. "You look so different."

"Different good?" asked Amy hopefully.

Emily kind of frowned. "I'm not sure."

"I think you look like a clown," said Carlie.

"Really?" Amy got worried now. What if Carlie was right? What if Amy had made a stupid mistake? More than anything else, Amy hated to look dumb.

"Look," said Morgan in a kinder tone. "You know we're your friends, don't you, Amy?"

"Of course." She nodded.

"Don't you think we'd be honest with you?"

"I, uh, I guess so."

"Well, that makeup is ... well, it's hard to get used to, Amy."

"I thought it looked pretty good this morning." Amy had actually thought it looked fairly glamorous too. And, combined with her new outfit and tall shoes, Amy thought that she should at least be able to pass for thirteen or fourteen now. She studied the faces of her friends now. Maybe they were jealous. After all, Amy had been the lucky one to receive a note from a boy — possibly from one of the most popular boys in their class. Or maybe they just wanted Amy to look way younger than them. Maybe they wanted her to be the baby of the group. Well, she was finished with that now! Amy stuck out her chin and held her head high and decided that her friends were simply envious. That had to be it.

"Hey," said Chelsea as she came over to join the group of girls.

Amy let out a little sigh of relief. Naturally, Chelsea would get this. "Hey," said Amy. "These guys are giving me a bad time about my makeup."

"Oh," said Chelsea, peering more closely at Amy. "You *are* wearing makeup. What's with that?"

"I just wanted to grow up a little," admitted Amy. "Do you think it looks okay, Chelsea?"

"I guess." She nodded, but didn't look completely convinced.

"Well, I think you could tone down that blue eye shadow some," said Morgan. "It seems a little over the top to me, Amy."

"I agree," said Emily.

"Me too," added Carlie.

Just then Amy saw several eighth grade girls walking by. They all had on eye shadow — and not so much different than hers. It seemed that her friends, well, other than Chelsea, were too unsophisticated to understand.

"I need to get to band," she told them.

"Hurry up," teased Carlie. "Maybe you can grab first chair before Oliver."

Seriously, her friends could act so immature at times. Still, Amy liked her friends. And she was glad to have her friends. She just wished they'd give her a little more respect. Now she wished she'd taken off her coat so they could've seen her whole new outfit. Surely, that would've impressed them a little.

"What happened to you?" asked Oliver as Amy entered the mostly empty band room.

She just shrugged and removed her damp coat, hanging it on one of the many pegs by the door. Who cared what Oliver Fitzgerald thought of her appearance anyway? He was actually wearing a bow tie today. Who did he think he was anyway — the host of the Miss America Pageant?

Oliver sat there staring at her as he adjusted the reed on his clarinet, but the expression on his face made her feel as if she'd sprouted a second head. "Man, Amy, you look like you got run over by a cosmetic truck."

She decided to ignore him as she sat down and slowly opened her clarinet case, taking her time to check her reed and clean her instrument.

Oliver continued to blab at her, saying how he didn't understand girls and fashion and why they went to so much trouble to "look perfectly ridiculous."

"Thanks a lot," she snapped at him. "Who died and promoted you to chief of the fashion police?"

He laughed. "Clever. At least your new airhead appearance hasn't destroyed any valuable brain cells yet."

With narrowed eyes, Amy put the clarinet to her lips and began to warm up. She wasn't about to let her rage toward stupid Oliver distract her from her music. One of these days she was going to unseat that ignorant boy, and then he'd be playing a new tune. In the meantime, it would take all her self-control not to unseat him by pushing him out of his chair and onto the floor right now. Wouldn't that be fun!

Even so, Amy stopped by the girls' restroom after band. She went directly to the mirror, trying to see what all the fuss was about. And as she looked at her image, she thought maybe her friends had been somewhat honest with her after all. As for Oliver — well, he was just mean. So Amy used a damp paper towel to rub off some of the blue eye shadow. Of course, that only messed up the mascara, making dark smudges beneath her eyes. She tried to fix it, but by the time the first warning bell rang, she wasn't sure if she'd made things better or worse. Maybe this whole makeup thing wasn't too smart after all. She tossed the paper towel into the trash and hurried out of the girls' restroom, nearly running smack into Brett Woods.

He stepped back startled. And, embarrassed, she said, "Oh, excuse me!" And then he actually smiled at her before he hurried on his way. Well, that wasn't too bad, she thought as she walked quickly to her next class. They hadn't exactly exchanged words yet, but it was a start. He had smiled!

"So, anything new developing with Brett?" Chelsea asked as they walked to the cafeteria together at noon. So Amy told Chelsea about bumping into him outside the restroom.

"It was kind of embarrassing," she confessed. "But I did say excuse me."

Chelsea laughed. "Well, that's one way to get him to speak to you."

"Well, he didn't actually *say* anything," admitted Amy. "Although he did smile at me."

"Why don't you let me talk to him for you?" said Chelsea eagerly. "Kind of move things along, you know?"

Amy wasn't sure. "I don't want him to think I'm being pushy."

"But what about the note?" Chelsea reminded her. "That's kind of pushy."

"But I'm not positive he wrote the note," said Amy. "I mean, it's really just a feeling. I don't know for sure."

"Well, I can find out," declared Chelsea. "And I'll be very diplomatic." Then she elbowed Amy, nodding toward the lunch line. "There he is. Just let me go and talk to him, okay?"

Amy shrugged then giggled. "Well, I guess I can't really stop you."

"That's right." Chelsea grinned. "This is going to be fun."

Suddenly Amy felt extremely nervous. "I'll go sit with Carlie and Emily," she said when she noticed those two were already at the table. "No way am I getting in the lunch line while you're talking to him."

"That's fine. I'll be right back." And then Chelsea took off.

And Amy headed straight for the table where her friends were just setting down their lunches. Seriously, Chelsea was not intimidated by anything. Amy knew for certain she wouldn't be able to walk up to a boy that she didn't even know and just start talking to him like that. Chelsea was a piece of work.

"Hello, Beautiful," teased Carlie as Amy sat down with her back to the lunch line. She did not want to see Chelsea talking to Brett. She did not even want to think about it.

"Hey, where's your lunch, Amy?" asked Emily. "Not hungry?"

So Amy quickly explained about Chelsea, and suddenly both Emily and Carlie were staring directly at the lunch line. All Amy could see was their expressions as they watched. "Is Chelsea talking to him yet?" she whispered as if she thought Brett might actually be listening to her.

"Oh yeah," said Emily quietly. "And he's talking to her too."

"And he's smiling too," said Carlie.

Amy so wanted to look. But at the same time, she didn't want Brett to see her watching. That seemed very uncool. "He's *really* smiling?" she asked quietly. "Like he's happy kind of smiling? Or nervous kind of smiling?"

"He seems happy. And he's talking to her and moving his hands," said Emily.

"And he's still smiling," added Carlie.

Funny how these two were suddenly so interested in all this. These girls who acted like they could care less about boys!

"They're still talking," said Emily. "And now they're laughing too."

"Can you believe Chelsea?" said Carlie, shaking her head. "No way would I just walk up to a boy and start talking to him like that."

"I wonder what she said to him," said Emily.

"Probably something like '*Amy Ngo likes you and she wants to know if you like her,*'" suggested Carlie in a sing-song voice. "I hear girls saying that kind of thing all the time. I think it's stupid."

"No," said Amy firmly. "She wouldn't say something that lame. She said she would be diplomatic."

"Diplomatic?" Emily laughed. "Like what's that supposed to mean?"

"It means she won't make me look dumb."

"You don't think this whole boy-crazy thing is a little dumb?" asked Carlie.

Amy let out an exasperated sigh. Would these girls ever grow up and get it? Maybe by high school.

"What's up?" asked Morgan as she joined them with

her lunch tray. "And why is Chelsea over there talking to a bunch of boys?"

So Emily and Carlie took turns explaining what was quickly beginning to feel like a three-ring circus to Amy.

"Here she comes," said Morgan.

"Looks like mission accomplished," said Emily.

Chelsea came to their table now, sitting down across from Amy with a deadpan expression.

"So, how did it go?" Amy asked nervously.

"Well ..." Chelsea frowned now. "It was both bad and good."

"Bad and good?" Amy felt confused. "Explain, please."

"The bad part was that Brett did not write that note, Amy."

"You asked him about the note?" Amy stared at her in shock. "You said you'd be diplomatic. I can't believe you brought up *the note*. Of course he'd deny it, Chelsea. He was in front of his friends. I can't believe you mentioned the note!" Amy felt sick. Why had she trusted Chelsea with something this important? This was wrong. All wrong!

chapter five

"So that's the thanks I get for going to talk to Brett for you?" asked Chelsea.

"You did it all wrong," said Amy.

"I thought you wanted to know if he was your secret admirer, Amy."

"But not like that."

"How else was I supposed to get to the bottom of it?"

"I don't know ..." Amy looked down at the table and sighed sadly. This was turning into a big fat mess.

"But you said part of it was good, Chelsea," pointed out Morgan. "Tell us the good part."

Amy looked up with a smidgeon of hope now. Was it possible that despite the fact that Brett hadn't written that note — or had denied it in front of his friends — that perhaps he liked her anyway? "Yeah," said Amy. "What was the *good* part?"

"Well, I guess it was more like good for *me* ..." Chelsea looked slightly uncomfortable now.

"Good for you?" demanded Amy. "What do you mean?"

Chelsea made a sheepish smile. "Well, it turned out that Brett wanted to get to know *me* better. He was actually glad that I came up and spoke to him."

"So you go up there and totally humiliate me by telling Brett Woods that I thought he was my secret admirer and then when he denies it — and why wouldn't he with all his friends looking on? — you go ahead and put the moves on him while you're at it?" Amy's embarrassment was quickly turning to anger now.

"I did NOT put the moves on him, Amy," said Chelsea. "I just talked to him, and we had a few laughs. I can't help it if he likes me."

"And I suppose you can't help it that you go over there to do me a favor, to talk to the boy I like, and then you end up stealing my guy right out from under my nose? And you think that's perfectly fine?" Okay, Amy knew she was being irrational, but this hurt. It hurt a lot.

"He wasn't *your* guy to steal, Amy."

"But you didn't know that."

"Come on, Amy," said Chelsea. "Don't be mad at me. Let's go get some lunch. He wasn't your secret admirer. It's no big deal."

"Maybe not to you." Amy stood now. "But it *is* to me. It's a big deal, Chelsea. You knew that I liked Brett, and you just went in there and flirted and took advantage of — "

"I did *not* flirt."

"You sort of did," said Carlie. "We were watching you."

"I was just being myself," said Chelsea defensively.

"It kind of looked flirty to me," said Emily.

"So you're taking Amy's side on this?" asked Chelsea in a hurt tone.

"No one's taking sides." Morgan let out a groan now. "See, this is what happens when you get all boy crazy, Amy."

"No," said Amy. "This is what happens when someone you trust betrays you."

"Amy," said Chelsea. "Brett's just not into you. I can't help that."

"No," said Amy again. "I guess you can't." Then she turned and walked away. Okay, she knew she was acting really stupid now. But she just couldn't help it. Then Amy headed for the girls' restroom, went into a stall, and actually cried. As silly as it seemed, she just cried. After a few minutes she came out and washed her face with cold water, removing the last traces of that stupid makeup. And, although she was hungry, she couldn't force herself to return to the cafeteria. Instead, she got an apple and some nuts from the snack machine and decided to go back to the band room to eat it. Mr. Barnett, the band teacher, always encouraged kids to practice there during lunch break, but usually no one took him up on it. Amy didn't intend to practice now. Mostly she just wanted a quiet getaway. And when she saw first chair empty, she decided to sit in it. Someday this chair was going to be hers anyway. She sat down and took a bite out of her apple, trying to figure out just where she'd gone wrong and what it would take to fixit.

"What's *your* problem?"

Startled to see that she wasn't alone, Amy looked up. And, naturally, Oliver Fitzgerald had decided to come to the band room today. Just great!

Amy narrowed her eyes at him without answering.

"Well, at least you washed your face," he said as she took the chair, second chair, next to her. "That's an improvement."

She turned and glared at him now.

"Really, Second Chair, you look much better without all that gloppity goop on — "

"Just shut up!" she said angrily. Then she stood, tossed her uneaten apple in the trash can by the door, and marched out of the band room, slamming the door behind her. She knew that she'd been incredibly rude, but she just didn't care.

Amy laid low for the rest of the day. Not only did she avoid Brett Woods, but she also managed to avoid her friends as well. And as soon as the final release bell rang, Amy hurried from her last class. Then, instead of going to their regular meeting place, at the end of the seventh grade locker bay, Amy made a quick exit and headed toward town. She knew her friends would wonder what had become of her, but she didn't care. She was too humiliated to care about anything.

Okay, as Amy slowly made her way toward town she decided she *did* care about a couple of things. 1) She cared that her feet were screaming in pain from these horrible, horrible shoes. She didn't know how other girls could stand them, and short or not, Amy did not intend to wear them again — ever! And 2) she cared about the fact that her stomach was growling with hunger. Amy was starving!

"What're you doing here?" snapped Ly as Amy slipped in the backdoor. She frowned at Amy's feet now. "And what are you wearing?"

"Don't even ask," said Amy. And suddenly tears were streaming down her cheeks.

Ly seemed to soften now. "What's wrong?" she asked in a surprisingly kind voice.

"I've had the worst day of my life," said Amy as she came into the kitchen. And then she removed the despised shoes and actually dumped them into the big trash can.

Ly put an arm around Amy's shoulders now. "Come with me," she said, guiding Amy toward the office. "Mom and Dad are meeting with the upholstery man, talking about getting the booths redone. An is out getting supplies, and Tu is out front, balancing the till after the lunch rush — it was Lyons Club Tuesday." Then she set Amy down in one of the easy chairs and opened the coat closet and rummaged around until she emerged with a pair of white canvas sneakers. "These might be a little big," she said as she handed them to Amy.

"Thanks." Amy sniffed as she slipped on the shoes, which turned out to be only about a half size too big.

"So, why is this your worst day ever?" asked Ly as she sat in the chair across from Amy.

Normally Amy didn't tell Ly too much about her life — mostly because Ly was usually too busy or too grumpy or too bossy. But suddenly Amy was pouring out the whole sad story. And as she told Ly, she almost expected her oldest sister to laugh — because in some ways it did sound a little silly. Or perhaps Ly might even scold Amy for being so foolish. But Ly just nodded and when Amy finally finished, she simply said, "I know how you feel, Amy."

Amy blinked. "You do?"

Ly nodded. "I don't have time to go into all of it right now, but I've been there too, Amy. I've experienced that same sort of thing myself."

"You have?"

"It's a hard lesson to learn ... that it's better just to be yourself, Amy. But in the end it's worth it."

Amy was stunned. But instead of questioning her sister, she just nodded.

"So, you missed lunch?" Ly stood now. "You must be starving."

"I am."

Soon, Ly returned with a plate heaped with food, which Amy quickly devoured. One thing about having a family restaurant — you didn't usually go hungry. And with a full stomach and feet that were no longer throbbing, Amy decided that maybe she was ready to walk home.

"Thanks, Ly," she said before she left. "For everything." Then to Amy's surprise, she actually hugged her sister. Ly looked surprised too, but she just smiled. Of course, in typical Ly-style she then rushed Amy out the backdoor, saying she had to get back to work now and reminding her to "be good!"

As Amy walked home she considered her day. On one hand, it had been lousy — totally a mess. She'd been humiliated in front of Brett Woods and his friends, finding out that he was not her secret admirer. By now she knew that when he'd smiled at her, he was probably actually laughing at her. The same way that stupid Oliver Fitzgerald had laughed at her. Even her own friends had questioned her "new look," which she was beginning to understand now. And then she'd gotten into a fight with Chelsea ... because she'd been jealous. Really, it was a nasty day that she never wanted to relive again. And yet being with Ly just now, hearing that she understood ... well, that was something.

Suddenly Amy remembered that today was supposed to be their homework afternoon. She wondered if the others were already there. She also remembered that she had promised to help Carlie with algebra. So, stopping off at home long enough to dump her backpack, change into comfortable clothes, and leave a note, Amy hurried on over to the clubhouse. She was surprised to see that no one was there yet. But she knew she had the day right. So she unlocked the door, went in and turned on the lights and the little heater, and made herself at home.

After a day like today, it felt particularly comforting to be back in the clubhouse. She just wished her friends were here too. She wanted to apologize to them — especially Chelsea — for acting like such a brat. After a while, she decided to put on a vinyl record. She thumbed through the stack of oldies (they had come with the bus) until she found a colorful old Beatles album called *Sgt. Pepper's Lonely Hearts Club Band*. She had to laugh at the title, since she felt like she could relate to being a "lonely heart." Maybe she should start a club herself, she thought as she put the needle carefully onto the record. And then after she played the song — and then played it again — she got an idea. And, as she played the song a third time, Amy's idea grew bigger. She would start her own Lonely Hearts Club!

"There you are!" declared Morgan as she and the

other girls piled into the bus and began peeling off jackets and backpacks, piling them here and there.

"Where have you been?" demanded Carlie, shaking her finger at Amy.

"Yeah, we've been looking all over for you," said Emily.

"I'm sorry," said Chelsea quietly. "I know you ran off because of me."

"No," said Amy. "I ran off because of *me*. I'm sorry too, you guys. I was really acting like a brat today. I mean, I thought I was being all grown-up and mature, but really I was acting like a big baby."

Soon they were all hugging and apologizing, and Amy felt mostly better. Okay, she was still a little irked at Chelsea and still a little hurt that Brett had denied being her secret admirer, but other than that, she was feeling more like her old self.

"And I got an idea," she announced as they began to sit down and get comfortable.

"An idea for what?" asked Morgan with interest.

So Amy told them about playing the old Beatles album and how it had affected her. "And so I have decided to create a Lonely Hearts Club myself," she told them.

"Huh?" Emily frowned. "What is that exactly? Like some kind of matchmaking service?"

"You don't mean something like those online dating

websites?" asked Morgan. "My mom has been threatening to try out one of the Christian sites, but I think it sounds totally freaky."

"No, nothing like that," Amy explained. "This is more like a *secret* club."

"A *secret* Lonely Hearts Club?" Carlie looked totally confused. "That sounds pretty creepy to me."

"Yeah, I have to admit that it sounds a little weird to me too," said Chelsea. "I mean, we all saw what happened today when I tried to help Amy with Brett. It got pretty messed up."

"Yeah, that was not cool," said Morgan. "Why would you want to do something like that—"

"No-no-no!" declared Amy. "You guys just don't get it. That's not the point!" Suddenly Amy felt discouraged all over again, like maybe this idea was just as lame as the makeup and shoes she'd worn to school today. Maybe Amy should learn to just lay low and keep her mouth shut. Certainly, that would be much less embarrassing than being teased by her friends!

chapter six

"So what is the point of this secret Lonely Hearts Club?" asked Emily after the bus had grown quiet and Amy was ready to completely abandon her idea. Really, what had she been thinking? Why did she think they would understand? She pressed her lips together and just frowned at her friends. She didn't want to talk. In fact, she was tempted to walk out just now.

"Come on, Amy," urged Morgan more softly. "Tell us. *What is the point?*"

"Fine!" Amy stood up now. "You'll probably just make fun of me all over again. But the point is there are a lot of sad people out there, people who have *lonely hearts.*"

"And?" Carlie nodded like she wanted Amy to continue.

"And I think they need to know someone cares about them."

"Yes," said Morgan with an encouraging smile. "That's a nice idea. Go on."

"Okay," said Amy. "There are people like my sister Ly. I was talking to her after school today, and I started to see her in a whole new way. I mean, sometimes I just think she's a big bossy grump, but suddenly I realized that maybe she's had her heart broken too. And I felt sorry for her. And I got to thinking about how it will be Valentine's Day next week, and there's all this focus on love and romance ... you know?"

"Yes," said Emily eagerly — like she understood. "Go on!"

"And, well, I wondered if some of those lonely hearts might actually be lonelier than usual. And I thought about how it felt kind of good to get a note from, you know, a secret admirer — I mean, even if it wasn't Brett Woods, it was still nice." Amy sighed. "So I thought maybe we could become sort of like secret admirers too — you know, for the people we know who might feel like lonely hearts on Valentine's Day."

"That's a fantastic idea!" said Emily, clapping her hands.

Amy blinked in surprise. "Really?"

"I love it!" said Carlie.

Morgan nodded with equal enthusiasm. "Me too! And we could even include my mom. She sometimes gets kind of sad around Valentine's Day too. Especially if she's not dating at the time, which is the case this year."

"And my mom is lonely too," added Emily quietly.

"And I was thinking about Miss McPhearson," said Amy. "Living by herself ... and we haven't been to see her since Christmastime."

"And how about Mrs. Hardwick down the street?" said Carlie. "Her husband died last year."

"And Mrs. Drimmel at the library," added Emily. "She's a widow too."

"And how about guys?" said Morgan. "Like Mr. Greeley."

"*Mr. Greeley!*" they all squealed at once.

"He would never admit it in a million years, but I know he'd love to get a secret admirer note!" exclaimed Emily.

"What about Mr. Hilliard?" suggested Chelsea. "He's single."

Emily laughed. "Yeah, and every girl in seventh grade has a crush on him, Chelsea. He probably already gets lots of secret admirer notes."

But more and more names were tossed out, and the enthusiasm for Amy's idea seemed to be steadily growing.

"So what will we do for all these lonely hearts?" said Carlie.

"Do we just write them each a secret admirer note?" asked Chelsea.

"That's a start," said Amy. "But I think we can do better than that."

"How about if we *make* them something?" suggested Morgan.

"Homemade valentines?" queried Emily.

"How about cookies too?" said Amy.

"And flowers," added Carlie.

And soon they had a complete plan. They would put together secret admirer valentine packs for every lonely heart they could think of. Chelsea offered to supply the heart-shaped pink boxes — she'd seen some with her mom at the craft store. Morgan would bring the valentine-making supplies. They would use Amy's kitchen to make cookies. And Emily would bring a book of poetry that they could use for transcribing onto the valentines. "Just in case we can't come up with something original for each one," she told them.

"Well, we better start by making a list," said Amy, grabbing for the notebook that Emily used for meeting notes. "You're the secretary, Emily. Want to write them down?"

So the girls all started throwing out names again. Even more this time than before. And between single or widowed neighbors and friends, family members, and teachers at school, the list grew longer and longer.

"What about kids at school?" said Amy suddenly. "I mean, most of our list seems to be for older people, which is great ... but what about kids like, well, like Susan Brinks."

Chelsea made a face. "That girl actually smells."

"That's not a very nice thing to say," said Morgan.

"But it's true. I have to sit next to her in home ec. And, believe me, I try to keep my distance."

"Exactly," said Amy. "Everyone tries to keep their distance from someone like Susan Brinks, which means she is probably really, really lonely. She needs a secret admirer more than anyone!"

"But how do we sneak our Lonely Hearts packages to kids at school without being seen?" asked Chelsea. "It's not like we can slip it into their lockers."

"Maybe we should do something smaller for kids at school," suggested Emily.

"Yes," said Amy. "Something like the note I found in my locker only more like a real valentine. But something that would slip between the vent slots."

"I'll make a separate list for those valentines," said Emily as she tore off another sheet of notebook paper.

So they all began tossing out even more names. And to Amy's dismay, even Oliver Fitzgerald's name wound up on their list. However, Amy decided that she'd let one of the other girls cover for him. No way was she going to send him a secret admirer's note!

"Wow," said Emily as she held up two nearly full pages of names. "There are a lot of lonely hearts in Boscoe Bay."

Although distracted with ideas for their Lonely Hearts Club, Amy reminded them of why they'd met this afternoon. "Remember homework and wanting to keep our grades up to get into Honor Society?" she said, nodding directly to Carlie now. "Didn't you want help with your algebra?"

And so, somewhat reluctantly, they set to doing homework. But before they finished up and went home, they decided to meet during the following weekend to put together their Lonely Hearts Club packages.

"We should plan on several hours to get it all done," said Morgan. "How about if we meet at one o'clock on Saturday and give it most of the afternoon?"

"And I'll check with my mom about baking cookies," said Amy as they walked back toward the mobile-home park.

Morgan slapped Amy on the back before they parted ways. "And really, Amy, the Lonely Hearts Club is a great idea."

"Yeah," agreed Emily. "Way to go."

Carlie gave her a high five. And Chelsea gave her a slightly nervous smile. "And so you're not mad at me anymore?" asked Chelsea in a cautious tone.

"Not really," said Amy. "But I'm not going to say it didn't hurt."

Then they all said good-bye and went their separate ways. Amy was thankful that Chelsea's mom was already there to pick her up. Otherwise, Amy would've felt like she should invite Chelsea to wait at her house. And, although Amy was working on forgiving Chelsea, she wasn't so sure she wanted to be alone with her just yet.

Amy unlocked the door and turned on the porch light. As usual, no one was at Amy's house during the dinner hour. She could see that her parents had been home, but by now they would be back at work. And she knew all she needed to do was to call and someone, probably An, would dash over and pick her up so she could spend the evening with them at the restaurant. But she was used to being on her own in the evenings. Plus, she needed to practice clarinet and finish up some homework. And, she was tired. It had been a long and exhausting day. Mostly she just wanted to forget all about it! At least the first half anyway. The second part had been much better.

Later that night, after her parents had gotten home and the lights were turned off and Amy was in bed, she thought about her old daydreams of going to the Valentine's Day dance and her silly hopes that Brett Woods would notice her and ask her to dance. Not only did that seem totally hopeless now, but to make matters worse, Amy realized that it was highly likely that Brett would invite Chelsea to dance with him! And instead of Amy floating off to the dance floor with the hottest guy in seventh grade, it would be Chelsea. And instead of Amy's friends being jealous of her, it would be Amy who would be jealous of Chelsea! Oh, why was life so unfair?

The next day, Amy decided to wear one of her new tops. But that was it. She was not wearing any of that stupid makeup. And she was definitely not wearing those ridiculous shoes which would probably be outside in the dumpster by now, due to be picked up by the garbage truck later today. Well, unless some dumpster diver found them. And they would be welcome to them!

Today, Amy just wanted to be herself. More than that, she did not want to be jealous of Chelsea. And she did not want to go around moping about Brett Woods. Still, it was a challenge once she got to school and saw Chelsea. She could tell that she was glancing around, trying to spot Brett, probably hoping that Brett was trying to spot her. And it grew into an even bigger challenge when Amy noticed Brett chatting with Chelsea outside the cafeteria right before lunch. Usually, Chelsea and Amy went into lunch together since their other friends always got there before them. Today Amy went alone.

"Where's Chelsea?" asked Emily when Amy set her tray down and joined her friends.

"Probably eating lunch with Brett-Baby," said Amy in a voice that sounded more bitter than she liked.

"Seriously?" Morgan made a face.

"Probably not," said Amy. "But they were talking."

"You couldn't pay me to eat lunch with a boy," said Carlie.

"Yeah," agreed Emily as she took a big bite out of her burger then talked with her mouth full. "That would totally ruin my appetite."

They laughed, but Amy was watching the door, waiting to see if Chelsea and Brett would come inside together. Surely they wouldn't actually eat lunch together. No one did that. Well, mostly no one. A few daring couples ate lunch together. But Amy agreed with Emily — eating with a boy would ruin her appetite too.

The four girls talked about their secret project. Morgan had already started to gather valentine-making supplies, and her grandma had given her a bunch of old packets of sequins and lace and things.

"This is going to be so fun," said Emily.

"And I know where a bunch of wildflowers are already starting to bloom," said Carlie. "I'll gather as many as I can right before Valentine's Day. We can tie them with a ribbon and stick them on top of the boxes."

"How are we going to deliver all these?" asked Emily suddenly.

"I think Grandma will help," said Morgan. "She really likes this idea, Amy. I told her you were the one who thought of it."

Amy smiled. "Thanks."

Then Chelsea and Brett walked into the lunchroom. Brett went to join his friends, and Chelsea came over to their table, pulling a rumpled paper sack from her backpack. "I'm brown-bagging it today."

"How's your boyfriend?" teased Carlie.

"He's fine,"said Chelsea a little too smugly.

"So, you really think of him as your boyfriend?" questioned Amy.

Chelsea nodded as she pulled out a Ziploc bag of carrot sticks. "Sort of. Is that a problem?"

Amy shrugged. "I guess not. Although I guess I hoped you'd wait a day or two … you know."

"But Amy, it's not like you guys were actually going together, remember?"

"I know." Amy nodded, trying to be mature.

"I agree with Amy," said Morgan. "Out of respect for her feelings, you could've waited a few days, Chelsea."

"Do you want me to break up with him?" asked Chelsea.

Amy wanted to say, "Yes, as a matter of fact, I do." But she just sat there.

"I will if you want me to, Amy."

"I don't really care," said Amy. "Do what you think is best."

"It might encourage you to know that Brett and I are trying to figure out who your secret admirer really is," said Chelsea as she took a bite of her sandwich.

Amy looked up in surprise. "Really?"

"Yeah. Brett thought maybe it was Tyler Epperson."

"Tyler Epperson?" Amy frowned. "Why him?"

"Brett thought it sounded like something Tyler might do. Besides that, Brett thinks that Tyler might like you."

"Oh no," said Carlie. "Here we go again. Boys, boys, boys! Seriously, Chelsea, can you just give it a break?"

"Yeah," said Emily. "Why don't you let poor Amy eat her lunch in peace today?"

"And the rest of us too," added Morgan.

But suddenly Amy felt interested. What if Tyler really did like her? Oh, he wasn't quite as good looking as Brett, but he wasn't exactly chopped liver either. And he was a pretty good friend of Brett's. And this might get her out onto the dance floor next week.

Suddenly, Amy held her hand up, shaping her thumb and little finger like a phone and mouthing the words *call me* to Chelsea. Naturally, Chelsea just grinned and nodded, and then the girls turned their conversation back to normal things — in other words, *not* boys. Instead, they talked about their Lonely Hearts project, which Amy was into. And then they talked about classes and whether or not they would go out for spring sports. Morgan and Carlie wanted to go out for track, but Emily and Chelsea thought softball would be more fun.

And, as usual, having a conversation about something besides boys did seem to make everyone happier. But, once again, Amy had to ask herself why it was that her friends were so resistant to having anything to do with boys — and why didn't they even seem to like talking to or about boys? And at the same time Amy admired them. And she even wished she could be more like them. Seriously, what good had it been for her to have that stupid crush — and then to be crushed by Brett Woods? And yet, Amy felt as if she was being pulled in again. Chelsea's suggestion that Tyler liked her was all Amy could focus on, all she could think about. She couldn't wait to talk to Chelsea and get the full story. But, at the same time, Amy wondered if she wasn't being a total idiot for wanting to know more about Tyler. So what if Chelsea and Brett thought he could be her secret admirer? It was probably more likely that he wasn't. And what if this ended up like it had with Brett? Or worse? What if Amy was the one who got hurt and humiliated all over again?

Seriously, how much more of that embarrassing nonsense could she even take? She was barely over Brett as it was. And, besides, who cared if dumb old Tyler Epperson "liked" her? What difference did it really make?

And yet, Amy knew she did care. She just didn't know why.

chapter seven

Later that day, Amy couldn't help but watch Tyler Epperson as he walked into English class. Although she was discrete, holding her assigned reading up just high enough that she appeared to be totally immersed in *The Jungle Book*. But, really, she was studying him. She noticed how his dark hair curled around his ears in a rather attractive way, and the way his long legs kind of folded under as he slipped into the seat diagonally across from her, just far enough in front of her that she could continue to take inventory without being observed. She liked his polo shirt — it was Ralph Lauren and neat and clean. And his shoes, Nike, were neat and clean as well. Okay, Tyler seemed like an okay guy. Maybe she should let Chelsea and Brett talk to him for her. Or maybe she was just setting herself up for another heartbreak. Oh, what was wrong with her?

"Okay, class," said Mrs. Murray. "Put down your reading and listen as I tell you about a special assignment."

Amy laid her book aside and sat up attentively. Even though she was often teased for playing teacher's pet, it was hard to give up old habits. Besides, she was one of those kids who really liked school. And she liked Mrs. Murray too.

"As you may know, next Tuesday is Valentine's Day and, for that reason, I have a special project. This will be a team project, and I want you to work in groups of four. But they must be mixed groups — with both girls and boys. I'm going to section you off into groups now, so there can be no arguing about who is in your group." Then Mrs. Murray worked her way around the room, counting off groups of four. And when she got to Amy, she included Tyler Epperson, along with Myrna Shaft and Bruce Jackson. After all the groups were selected, Mrs. Murray began disbursing what appeared to be a play.

"Your group of four will read through this play together, each with an assigned role, but as you will see, the play seems to stop halfway through. The way your play concludes will be up to you. You and your team will write the ending of the play, each person taking responsibility for the role that he or she is playing. But you must work together."

There were some groans as well as some sounds of interest. Amy actually thought it sounded like a fun assignment, and she couldn't believe her luck of getting to be with Tyler. She wasn't too sure about Myrna and Bruce though. In Amy's opinion, those two weren't the smartest kids in the class — and that was an understatement. Still,

Amy was used to working with kids who weren't equal to her academically. Wasn't that the story of her life?

"Go ahead and break into your groups now. First you can assign your roles and then you can take turns reading your parts. It might be helpful to choose a director for your production, but I will leave that up to you. Tomorrow and Friday you will have time to write your endings, and on Monday you can practice and make revisions before you turn in your finished plays. I will read and judge the plays, choosing first-, second-, and third-place winners." She smiled at the class. "And, of course, there will be prizes."

Everyone clapped now. Amy did the math — that meant twelve prizes would be awarded, and that was nearly half of the class. Her chance at getting one seemed pretty good.

"And the first-place winners will also be invited to perform their play for the entire class on Valentine's Day. Now go ahead and spread out in the room as you break into your groups. And good luck!"

Amy glanced shyly at Tyler now. She was used to being the kind of student who took charge in group projects, and everything in her wanted to be the director. But at the same time she didn't want to appear too bossy.

"Why don't we go over there," he said, nodding to a corner of the room that no one had taken yet.

"Great," said Amy with a bright smile. "You guys

coming?" she asked Myrna and Bruce, and they just nodded as they gathered up their stuff and followed.

"Okay," said Tyler. "Who wants to be director?"

"Not me," said Bruce.

And Myrna just shook her head.

"I'm willing," admitted Amy. "Only if no one else wants to."

Tyler nodded. "Go for it."

And so Amy did. She had already glanced over the script and knew which were the lead roles (Kent and Alice), and she assigned them to Tyler and herself. The secondary roles (Jon and Marion) she assigned to Bruce and Myrna. "And now let's take turns reading through it," she told them.

The story was about four grown-up friends who had gone to high school together and were at their tenth reunion. They were all married to other people, but Kent and Alice had been high school sweethearts and Jon and Marion had been their best friends. It was actually a fairly boring play, and Amy suspected that their teacher may have written it herself. But just the same, Amy was interested in remaking the ending so that she and Tyler (rather Kent and Alice) would be reunited once again. But she also knew she'd have to go about this carefully. Fortunately, the bell rang just as they finished reading their parts, and she told them all to think about the ending of the play and that they would work on it tomorrow.

"Yeah, right," said Tyler in a way that suggested he had no plans to think about it at all.

Amy just grinned. "Well, then you better watch out, Tyler, or we just might write your character into a corner or even kill him off."

Bruce and Myrna laughed, and Tyler looked surprised. Then Amy, feeling pleasantly in control, gathered up her things and walked off. At least she'd given that boy something to think about!

It wasn't until later that afternoon that Chelsea called her. And Amy couldn't wait to tell Chelsea about Tyler being in her production group.

"Wow, that is so cool," said Chelsea. "Did he choose to be in it?"

"Well, no. Mrs. Murray assigned us. But he seemed okay."

"I wish I had Mrs. Murray for English. That sounds like a fun assignment."

"The fun will be creating a totally romantic ending," said Amy in a dreamy voice. "I want Tyler, oops, I mean Kent, to fall in love with Alice. That's my character."

"And then maybe life will imitate art, and Tyler will fall in love with you?"

"Exactly!" Amy laughed.

"Sounds like a good plan."

Just then Amy heard Ly calling. "I've got to go now.

It's my night to hostess at the restaurant." Amy hung up and hurried out to get into Ly's car.

"How's life?" Ly asked as they drove to town.

"Great," said Amy. Then she told Ly the same story she'd just told Chelsea.

But Ly's reaction was nothing like Chelsea's. "Oh, Amy," said Ly in a disappointed tone.

"What's wrong?" asked Amy.

"What's *wrong*?" Ly glanced at her. "You just told me how badly you were hurt when that other boy didn't like you, Amy. And now here you go again."

"Are you saying that just because Brett doesn't like me I should give up on boys completely?"

Ly didn't say anything.

"Is that what *you* did, Ly?"

Ly just shrugged as she pulled into the parking lot behind the restaurant.

"Is that what happened to you, Ly?" persisted Amy.

"All I'm trying to say, Amy ..." Ly turned off the car. "Is that I don't want to see you getting hurt."

"I know ..." Amy got out of the car and looked at her sister. "And, trust me, I don't want to get hurt either."

"Okay ..." Ly nodded.

"But I don't want to hide from living my life either," said Amy.

Ly didn't say anything as they walked to the back

door. But Amy hoped that she got the message, because Amy felt certain that Ly was hiding from life. But as they went inside, Amy considered what Ly had said to her too. Maybe Ly was partially right. Maybe it was a little silly for Amy to be chasing after another boy again.

The next day was sunny, so Amy walked with her friends to school. They were happily discussing their valentine project — the Lonely Hearts Club that had actually been her idea — but Amy was distracted. It seemed like her mind had gotten stuck — all she could think about was Tyler Epperson and how she planned to direct their English assignment later that day. And how she hoped she could direct him into playing the leading love interest.

"Earth to Amy!" said Morgan loudly.

"Very funny," said Amy. "Why don't you come up with a new one?"

"Why are you so spacey?" asked Emily.

"She's probably thinking about boys again," said Carlie.

"Which boys?" asked Morgan.

"Give me a break," said Amy.

"Amy should've gone to church with us last night," said Emily.

"Yeah," agreed Morgan. "The sermon was about our minds."

"What about our minds?" asked Amy, eager to get them talking about something besides her.

"Pastor George said that we can either control our minds or our minds can control us."

"What's that supposed to mean?" asked Amy. "I thought our minds did control us."

"They sort of do," explained Emily. "But when you're a Christian you want Jesus to be in control. You want him to lead you and show you better ways to think."

"For instance," said Morgan. "What were you so distracted about just now, Amy?"

Amy didn't want to admit it.

"See, it was boys," teased Carlie.

"Fine," said Amy. "I was thinking about a boy." And then she told her friends about Tyler Epperson. And it was actually a relief to have it out in the open. Except that it was kind of embarrassing too.

"Okay," said Morgan. "Do you think that the thoughts you had about Tyler were inspired by Jesus or by yourself?"

Amy considered this then frowned. "Probably myself."

"Is that sort of how it was with Brett?" asked Emily. "Did you think about him a lot?"

Amy wanted to say "duh,"but controlled herself and simply nodded.

"And where did that get you?" asked Morgan.

"Nowhere," admitted Amy.

"Worse than nowhere," pointed out Carlie."It made you miserable. We saw you, Amy. You were a mess."

"Yeah." Amy sighed. "You're right."

"So, just think about it," said Morgan. "Do you want Jesus to lead you and help you keep your mind on things that are good for you? Or do you want to just let your mind wander down any old back alley?"

"Where you could get mugged," added Emily.

"I see your point," said Amy.

"And it's really simple," said Morgan. "You just need to pray and ask Jesus to lead you ... just ask him to change your ways of thinking so that you're more like him."

"Like when you got that Lonely Hearts Club idea," said Carlie. "I think that Jesus must've helped you with that one."

"And that's what we were just talking about," said Emily.

"While you were zoning," added Morgan.

"Sorry," said Amy. "By the way, my mom said it was fine to use our kitchen to make cookies."

"Great," said Morgan. "Everything seems to be coming together!"

As they went into the school, Amy tried to replay the mini-sermon that Morgan and Emily had just given her. In some ways it made sense. And it was true that Amy wasn't that comfortable when her mind started to obsess over Tyler. She knew it didn't even make sense. For one thing, she barely knew the boy. For another thing, she really didn't want to be totally humiliated again. And so, just as she thought she was getting a handle on this, she saw Tyler and Brett walking by, and it seemed that her friends' words just vanished in a puff of smoke.

chapter eight

"Okay, this is what I found out," whispered Chelsea as she and Amy exited the cafeteria after lunch. "Tyler thinks you're nice and smart."

"He said that?"

Chelsea nodded happily. "And I can tell by the way he said it that there's something more behind it, Amy. I think he really likes you!"

Amy let out a happy squeal.

"So, let me know how English goes," said Chelsea.

"Absolutely," said Amy.

Now Amy couldn't wait for her last class of the day. In fact, it made it hard to focus during her other two classes. As a result, she made a stupid mistake on the chalkboard during Algebra Two.

"Way to go, Second Chair," teased Oliver as Amy returned to her desk feeling completely humiliated. "Can't keep your mind on the numbers today, eh?"

Naturally, she ignored him. But, even as she did, she couldn't help but remember what Morgan and Emily had told her earlier. And she had to ask herself—just who was controlling her thoughts now?

Finally, it was English, and she got to sit right next to Tyler as they plotted the ending of their play. Amy was glad that Myrna and Bruce didn't seem to care how the play ended, as long as someone else did the work. That was fine with Amy.

"You're really good at this, Amy," said Tyler as the class ended. "I'm glad I got to be in your group."

"You had some great ideas too," said Amy. "I liked how you had Kent talking about being the big football hero in high school and then just an overweight soccer coach as an adult."

Tyler laughed. "I have an uncle like that."

"Well, we only need a couple more scenes to wrap it up," said Amy. "Maybe we can finish it tomorrow, then I can do the editing on it and print it out during the weekend."

Tyler gave her a high five. "Sounds good!"

Amy was hoping that Tyler would continue walking with her as they exited the classroom, but he took off toward his friends and she walked by herself to the locker bay. At her locker, she stopped to unload a couple of things from her backpack when she noticed a piece of paper sticking out of a zippered pocket. She pulled out the paper to discover it was another secret admirer note!

Dear Amy,

The more I know you, the more I like you. Not only are you the prettiest and smartest girl in the school, you are pretty funny too!

YSA

Amy looked over her shoulder like she expected the writer of the note to pop out and say, "Hey, it's me!" But all she saw was Emily and Morgan walking her way. She smiled and waved. And then she showed them the note.

"So the mystery continues," said Emily with real interest.

"You're good at mysteries," said Amy. "Who do you think it is?"

Emily took the note and peered carefully at it. "Well, it does seem to be a boy."

"Duh," said Morgan.

"And he has neat handwriting. Does the style look familiar to you, Amy?"

Amy studied the note more closely. "Well, now that you mention it, Tyler's handwriting actually looks kind of like that. And—" she looked at her friends with a rush of excitement. "He was using a pen this exact same color in English."

"It's blue," said Morgan in a flat tone.

"But it's kind of a purple blue," said Amy.

"You're right," said Emily. "It is."

"And—" gushed Amy, "whoever wrote this note had to have been near me this afternoon because I found it in my backpack!"

"Good point," said Emily. "Did Tyler have an opportunity to slip it into your backpack during English?"

"I did get up to put something in the trash," Amy told them. "It was a scene that we decided didn't work. He could've slipped it in then."

"Slipped what in?" asked Chelsea. She had just joined them. So Amy filled her in on the latest Secret Admirer news.

"Cool," said Chelsea. "That has to be it."

"Well, don't let it go to your head," warned Morgan.

"And don't forget what we told you this morning," said Emily.

"I'm trying to keep that in mind," said Amy. "But it's not easy." She giggled. "It's hard not to think about boys when boys are thinking about you!"

Chelsea laughed and slapped Amy on the back. "You go, girl."

But Morgan just shook her head, and Emily looked concerned. And when Carlie joined them, and heard about Amy's second note, she rolled her eyes.

"Oh, great," said Carlie, "here we go again."

"Does anyone want to go shoe shopping with me?" Chelsea asked. "I realized that I don't have the right shoes to go with my Valentine's Day dance outfit."

Morgan, Emily, and Carlie all declined Chelsea's offer, but Amy said she'd go. "As long as your mom can drop me off at the restaurant by five."

"No problem," said Chelsea.

So Amy called the restaurant on her cell phone and told An what her plans were for after school.

"No homework?" asked An.

"Not much," said Amy. "I can do it later."

"Okay then ..."

And so, Amy and Chelsea were chauffeured around in the Mercedes, and all they talked about as they shoe-shopped was boys — specifically Brett and Tyler. By the time Amy was dropped off at Asian Garden, she felt certain that Tyler had been her secret admirer all along.

"I thought he acted weird when I asked Brett about it," Chelsea had finally told Amy. "He had this uncomfortable look in his eye, you know, like *you've got the wrong guy*. You've got to help break the ice with him, Amy. Somehow you need to let him know that you got the note and that you feel the same way about him."

Of course, Amy wasn't quite sure how she was going to accomplish this. And as she helped with hostess duties and seating people at tables, she ran a few possibilities through her head. But nothing seemed quite right.

It wasn't until she was getting ready for bed that she came up with a solution. If Tyler liked sending notes, perhaps she should send him one as well. And, like him, she would call herself a "secret admirer."

Amy got out her best pink stationery and attempted to

pen a note. And, after several tries, she finally decided to keep her note brief. Just get to the point without revealing who she was — just in case she was wrong about Tyler being her secret admirer. No way did she want to set herself up for any more public humiliation, and she'd made Chelsea promise not to mention the notes to ANY of the boys this time.

Dear Tyler,
Thank you for the notes.
I really like them. And I really like you.
♥ YSA

Then she put her note inside a pink envelope and sealed it. Okay, she wasn't exactly sure how she would get it to him. His backpack? Or his locker? But she could figure that out tomorrow.

As Amy walked with her friends to school, she tried to pretend she was listening to all they said. She nodded and said, "Uh-huh," at appropriate times, but all she could really think about was the pink envelope in her backpack. She had decided to tell no one about this. It would be her secret. Then, just in case Tyler wasn't the one who'd written her — although she felt 99 percent sure that he was — she wouldn't be embarrassed again.

"Amy is daydreaming about boys again," said Carlie as they turned into the schoolyard.

"What?" Amy turned and looked innocently at Carlie.

"Don't try to hide it," said Emily. "We know."

Morgan nodded. "Yeah, we know."

"And it's starting to worry us," said Carlie.

Amy shrugged. "Sorry."

"Hopefully you won't be the one who's sorry," said Morgan.

"Why should I be sorry?" asked Amy.

"Because you're missing out," said Carlie. "You're living in La-La Land, as my dad would say."

"And we miss you," said Emily.

Amy smiled at her friends. "You guys are imagining things."

"Hey, what's going on up there?" asked Carlie, pointing to where a bunch of kids were clustered in the courtyard.

"Looks like a fight," said Morgan.

Amy glanced at her watch now. "Well, I gotta get to band. See ya!" And she took off through the seventh grade locker bay.

She hadn't expected to have an opportunity to drop off her note just now, but to her surprise the locker bay was empty — probably due to whatever was going on in the courtyard just now. Anyway, Amy knew this was her big chance. And she also knew which locker was Tyler's. She had figured that out yesterday while spying on him.

So she casually walked past the guys' side of the bay and then paused very briefly in front of a certain locker as she slipped the pink envelope right through a vent slot. And then, feeling like a criminal, she hurried away. By the time she reached the band room, her heart was pounding so hard she thought someone might mistake it for a snare drum.

She was actually earlier than usual, and she was relieved to see that Oliver wasn't there yet either. She did not need him teasing her again just now. She hung up her jacket, went to her seat, and casually began to warm up on her clarinet. It was amazing how soothing it was simply to play the scale. It settled her nerves, and before long she nearly forgot all about the pink envelope.

Oliver grinned at her as he came into the band room. "Hey, you beat me this morning, Second Chair. I guess I better be watching out."

She simply rolled her eyes and continued to warm up.

By the time class ended, Amy felt completely at ease about her secret note. She figured this would be a win-win situation. Either Tyler would reveal himself to her, and she would know that she'd hit the nail on the head — and they would be dancing together by the time of the Valentine's Day dance. Or, nothing would happen, and Amy would know that Tyler hadn't been her secret admirer after all. And it was weird that in some ways Amy would be relieved if that was the case. She hated to admit it, but she was starting to understand why her friends, other than Chelsea, seemed happier without being boy crazy. Maybe there was a reason people called it "boy crazy" — maybe it actually did make you crazy!

"There she is!" said a guy's voice. Amy looked up to see a short, blond guy she didn't know standing with Tyler and several other seventh grade boys, including Brett. And the guy was pointing right at her. "That's the girl who put that stupid note in your locker, Tyler."

Amy wanted to disappear. She wanted the wooden floors to open up and swallow her whole. She felt her face getting hot as the boys came closer to her.

"Did you write this?" demanded Tyler, waving the way too familiar pink envelope and note in front of her nose.

Amy didn't answer. She just looked down at her feet and wondered why they had forgotten how to move.

"Because if you think I like you," he continued loudly, "if you think I'm going to be your boyfriend, you are totally crazy!"

"Hey," said Oliver, stepping between Amy and Tyler now. "Back off, bud."

Oliver, though skinny, was several inches taller than most of the seventh-grade boys, and for some reason the guys seemed to be taking him seriously just now.

"Well, I don't want you putting stuff in my locker, Amy!" shouted Tyler from behind Oliver. "So knock it off, ya hear!"

"She can hear you already," said Oliver in a calm yet firmvoice. "Now why don't you and your buddies just clear out." He shook his head. "It's a pretty bad state of affairs when guys have to pick on girls for their kicks."

The boys made some grumbles and tossed out a few mean comments, but they slowly dispersed. And suddenly Amy's feet remembered how to move, and without even saying a word, she took off in the opposite direction and ran.

She wasn't really sure where she was going, but she knew she wanted to get out of there. And so she ran and she ran until she ended up in town ... in front of her family's restaurant. Of course, they weren't open this early in the day, but she knew that someone would be inside. She just hoped that it wasn't her parents. Usually her parents didn't come in until eleven.

"What are you doing here?" demanded Ly when Amy slipped in the backdoor. "Why aren't you at school?

"Amy," said An as she set down a big chopping knife. "What's wrong?"

And so Amy told both her sisters the whole story about what a fool she'd been. To her dismay they both started to giggle, and then they were both laughing — hysterically!

"It's not funny!" said Amy.

"It's a little funny," said Ly as she leaned into An's shoulder, suppressing her laughter.

"Well, I'm glad that I can entertain you both!" Amy stomped her foot now.

"We're sorry," said An. She stepped over and put her arm around Amy. "But I do think we both needed a good laugh just now."

"Yes, thank you," said Ly.

"We were actually having a fairly serious discussion about guys and relationships," said An.

"And you provided some good comic relief," said Ly.

"Glad you enjoyed my pain," said Amy in grumpy voice.

"But why did you leave school?" asked An.

"Because I'm too humiliated to go back."

"You have to go back," said Ly.

"I can't," said Amy.

"You don't have a choice," said An, placing a firm hand on Amy's shoulder. "You have to go back. Do you want me to take you?"

"No." Amy firmly shook her head. "I can take myself."

"You'll need to check in at the office now," said Ly. "And explain why you were truant."

"Truant?" Amy frowned. She didn't like the sound of that word.

Ly nodded. "Yes. That's what they call it."

"Fine," said Amy. "I'm going."

"This is one of those times when you need to ask God to help you, Amy," said An. "He wants us to call out to him in times of trouble."

"Right," said Amy. "That would be now."

"So, *do* that," said An. "Call out to God, and he will answer you."

Amy didn't say anything as she headed for the back door.

But she knew this — she was not going back to school today.

Maybe never again!

chapter nine

Amy's feet seemed to know just where to go as she exited the restaurant. Apparently, they were taking her directly home. But then, as she entered the mobile-home park, it occurred to her that she would have to face her parents here. Facing her siblings was one thing, but facing her parents — particularly her mother — well, that was something else.

And so Amy made a beeline to the clubhouse. She knew it was wrong and that she would be considered "truant," as Ly had pointed out. And Amy knew she would probably be punished later when her parents found out, but she just didn't care. It felt as if there was a big aching hole in her chest, and she no longer cared about school or being in trouble or even her friends. Amy was desperate.

She unlocked the door and let herself inside and then she went to the back of the bus, flopped down onto the bed, and began to sob. Oh, why had she been so incredibly dumb? Why had she written that stupid note? Why had she allowed herself to become boy crazy like this? What was wrong with her? Why couldn't she be more like Morgan and Emily and Carlie? They didn't have problems like this. For a supposedly "smart girl" Amy felt like a complete idiot!

She must've cried herself to sleep because when she opened her eyes it was already twelve. Her friends would be in the cafeteria now. They were probably wondering where she was — and they'd probably heard the story of Tyler confronting her outside the band room. It was so humiliating!

Amy got up and looked at herself in the little mirror that was attached to the tiny closet. Her face was flushed, and her eyes were puffy from crying. And she almost looked like she was sick. Perhaps she could convince her parents that she'd come home sick. But then again, her sisters already knew. And she hadn't exactly gone home either.

"What am I going to do?" she said, feeling more desperate than ever. Then she remembered what An had told her — about calling on God. And it became very clear that was what she needed to do. She got down on her knees next to the bed and, closing her eyes, she begged God to help her.

"I've been a stupid girl," she said aloud. "I tried to figure things out on my own, God. I never even asked for you to help me. I didn't ask for you to show me the way I should go, I just stumbled through on my own and now I have made a complete mess." More tears came now. "I'm so sorry, God," she sobbed. "I know how much I need you. I know I was stubborn and stupid. I left you totally out of things and went my own ignorant way. Please, forgive me. And, please, help me to get back on track with you. I really, really don't want to be boy crazy anymore. I really, really want to live my life the way you want me to live it. I want to be more like Morgan and Emily and Carlie, God. I want to follow you. Please, help me."

She prayed like that for a long time, and when she finally said, "amen," she felt a strange sort of calm and peace. And then she felt hope. Real hope. And this wasn't that kind of silly hope — like maybe some stupid boy liked her — no, this was a deep, solid hope — a reminder that God loved her. God loved her! What more did she need?

Amy got her backpack and went to her house. To her surprise, her mom was still there.

"Amy?" said Mom with a shocked look. "What are you doing home at this time of day?"

"I have to tell you something," said Amy. And then, just like that, Amy told her mother the whole story. And her mother just sat there and listened.

"I'm sorry," Amy finally said. "I know that I did stupid things and I know I shouldn't have left school. But I was so humiliated. And then An and Ly laughed at me ... and I just couldn't make myself go back to school."

"Your sisters laughed at you?" asked her mother with a creased brow.

"Not in a mean way," Amy said quickly. "It's just that they were having some big talk about guys and stuff, and I caught them off guard. But I've decided that I never want to be boy crazy again, Mom. I know I am way too young for that stuff. And all it does is hurt and make a mess of things."

Mom smiled and nodded. "It sounds like you are growing up, Amy."

"Really?"

"Those are wise words for a girl your age."

"Well, I used to think I was so smart," confessed Amy. "But now I know I'm not as smart as my friends, because Morgan and Emily and Carlie kept telling me that I was making a mistake to be boy crazy. They're not like that at all. And they said I'd probably get hurt. And they were right."

"You have wise friends too."

"So, are you going to punish me?" asked Amy.

Her mom just looked at her now. "I think you've punished yourself enough."

Amy nodded.

"But I am going to take you back to school now."

Amy frowned. "I was afraid of that."

So Amy's mom drove her back to school, went with

her to the office, and after a quick explanation, which thankfully wasn't too specific, Amy's absence was actually excused. Amy went to Algebra Two, getting there just before the tardy bell rang.

Today, she gave the math problems her complete concentration. And today she didn't make any mistakes on the chalkboard. She focused all her attention on her assignment and even managed to finish up by the time the bell rang. Oh, she knew that her last class of the day would be English and she would have to face Tyler. She knew it wouldn't be easy, but she simply wanted to get it over with.

To her surprise, when she got to English, Tyler acted almost as if nothing had happened earlier today. Sure, he wasn't a bit friendly, and he seemed as uncomfortable as she felt, but somehow the four of them managed to work on their play, and eventually came up with an ending that seemed okay. It wouldn't win any prizes, but at least it wasn't romantic. No way did Amy want a romantic ending to this stupid play.

And the whole time Amy was careful not to look Tyler in the eyes. That would be too embarrassing! She mostly kept her head down, carefully writing down the lines that they came up with. Still, it seemed like a very long class. And finally, without looking directly at Tyler, she promised her group that she'd come back on Monday with a printed out script for everyone. When the last bell rang, Amy practically leaped out of her seat and ran from the room. She couldn't ever remember being this glad to see a school day end. And thank goodness it was Friday! She would have two whole days to recover from today's humiliation.

"Amy, where were you at lunch today?" Morgan asked as Amy's four friends surrounded her in front of her locker.

"I'll tell you on the way home," she said quietly as she rearranged her backpack and slammed her locker shut. All Amy wanted right now was to get out of this school and away from any more possibly humiliating scenes.

"We decided to start work on the Lonely Hearts valentines today," said Emily as they headed for the exit. "We're all going to the clubhouse now."

"That way we can work all afternoon," said Morgan. "Can you come too?"

"Just until five," Amy told her. "Then I have to be at the restaurant. It's Friday, you know, and they get busy."

"That's fine."

"So, why did you decide to do it today instead of tomorrow?" Amy took a deep breath as they got outside. Soon they would be away from school ... away from guys like Tyler or Brett — or any more curious glances.

"We want the valentines to be completely finished by Saturday," explained Carlie.

"Because we found out that we have to work on decorations for the dance on Monday after school," Chelsea informed her. "Vanessa said it would take us several hours."

"And we want the valentines all ready to deliver on Tuesday morning *before* school," said Morgan.

"My mom and Morgan's grandma are going to help with the driving," said Chelsea.

"Wow," said Amy. "Sounds like you guys have it all worked out."

"We had an emergency planning meeting at lunch," said Morgan.

"We missed you," said Carlie.

Amy nodded, looking at her friends. "I missed you guys too."

"We heard about what happened by the band room this morning," said Emily in a quiet voice, almost like she didn't want to bring the whole thing up.

Amy sighed. "Yeah ... I figured everyone probably knows by now."

"I told them about it," admitted Chelsea. "But only because Brett told me the whole thing and I felt so sorry for you."

"You must've been pretty embarrassed," said Carlie. "I think I would've died if something like that happened to me."

"It was like a bad dream," Amy told them. Then, as

they walked home, she replayed the whole thing, how she had left the school grounds, been laughed at by her sisters, and even how she'd hidden out at the clubhouse.

"Wow," said Carlie. "I never would've believed that Amy Ngo would actually play hooky from school."

"That's not like you at all, Amy," said Morgan with wide eyes.

Then Amy told them about praying to God and how it seemed like he'd answered and how she actually felt hopeful when she was done. "It's like something in me really changed," she finally said. "Like I really got it. I mean, one moment I felt hopeless and upset ... and then it was like a miracle, I felt like I could deal with things."

"We were so worried about you," said Emily. "We were all praying for you today."

"Thanks," said Amy. "I totally appreciate it."

"So, are you okay now?" asked Carlie with a worried expression.

Amy smiled at all of them. "I am okay. I mean, sure, I'm really embarrassed that I was such an idiot and that everyone saw me being publicly humiliated. It was pretty horrible. And you guys all know how I don't like to look stupid."

"Do we ever!" said Morgan. "We didn't used to call you *Miss Ngo It All* for nothing."

Amy sort of laughed. "Well, now I can admit that I do *not* know it all. In fact, it feels like I don't know much of anything. Especially when it comes to boys!"

chapter ten

On Saturday afternoon, they were just finishing up their Lonely Hearts project. Amy and Carlie had been the baking team, making several batches of Amy's mom's recipe of almond cookies. Emily had been printing out the valentine greetings that she had found in poetry books. Chelsea and Morgan had been decorating the Valentine's Day cards and the boxes, and now they were all working to assemble the packages.

Amy stepped back to admire the valentines, all stacked along the couch in the clubhouse like a small mountain of pretty pink hearts.

"They are so beautiful," she said to her friends as she wrapped another set of cookies in plastic wrap, tying it with a pink ribbon before she handed it off to Morgan.

"We could probably sell them if we wanted to," said Carlie. "Not that we'd want to, of course."

"I've worked out the delivery lists," said Emily as she held up the notebook. "But I'm a little concerned about delivering to Miss McPhearson. You know how it takes awhile to get out to her house. All the other deliveries are either in Harbor View or town or school."

Amy considered this. Miss McPhearson was Amy's special friend, and Amy knew that the old woman would probably feel badly if someone came out and made a delivery but didn't come in to say hello.

"It's going to be hard to get out there and back in time for school on Tuesday morning," pointed out Morgan.

"Maybe I could get An to take me out to deliver it to her tomorrow," said Amy. "I know it's early, but that way I could spend a little time with her too. You know how lonely she is."

"That's for sure," said Carlie. "Of all the lonely hearts, Miss McPhearson could be the queen."

"Queen of the Lonely Hearts," said Emily.

"So, does anyone want to come with me?" asked Amy. "I think I could talk An into taking us after church, but we go to early church, you know, so that we can get to the restaurant on time for the after-church rush."

As it turned out, the others wouldn't be out of church on time, and Chelsea and her parents had plans.

"We're done," said Morgan finally.

"Cool," said Carlie.

"I just have once question," said Amy. "Uh, who is going to put the valentines into kids' lockers at school?"

Morgan laughed. "Meaning that you don't want to?"

Amy firmly shook her head.

"I don't blame her," said Chelsea. "Not after Friday."

"Here's an idea," said Emily. "Since Morgan's grandma and Chelsea's mom are helping to make deliveries, maybe Carlie and I can go to school early and sneak the other valentines into lockers before kids are around to see. And Amy, you don't have to if you don't want to."

"I can help Morgan and her grandma deliver valentines," offered Amy.

Soon it was all settled, and Amy was relieved that there would be no chance of her getting caught slipping a valentine into someone's locker.

"I just thought of someone we didn't send a valentine to," said Emily suddenly. "And he's a pretty lonely guy too."

"Who?" they all asked.

"Derrick Smith."

Carlie groaned. "Derrick Smith? He's the biggest jerk in school."

Amy couldn't help but agree. Derrick Smith had only recently returned from being incarcerated in juvenile detention. He'd been the meanest of the bullies last year, and no one liked him.

"I know," said Emily. "He's been a pain. But I think it's because he's in pain too."

"Emily is right," said Morgan. "We have to make a valentine for Derrick too."

So they all set to work making one more valentine. But

then there was a brief argument over who would deliver it. Finally, Emily said she would.

"I just hope you don't get spotted," Amy warned her.

"I'll be very careful," said Emily.

Then the girls finished up, locked the bus, and Amy went home in time to be picked up by Tu to go to work at the restaurant. Saturday was always a busy night for them, and it wasn't unusual for kids from school to come to Asian Garden with their parents. But Amy was not prepared to see Tyler and his family there celebrating, as it turned out, his mom's birthday. And it was too late for Amy to run and find someone else to see them to their table. And so she held her head high and pretended that Tyler hadn't seriously hurt her feelings just yesterday as she showed them to the table and took their drink orders. But as she did this she managed to totally ignore Tyler, pretending like she didn't even know him.

"What a nice young lady," Tyler's dad said as Amy left the table. Of course, he couldn't see her rolling her eyes as she hurried away, begging An to take over for her.

"Table seven?" said An with surprise. "That's the boy who was mean to you?"

Amy nodded. "Please, don't make me go back in there."

"I'll handle it," said An. Then she winked. "Want me to slip something into his tea?"

Amy chuckled. She knew An was joking, but it was pretty funny. Still, Amy was relieved when An offered to take over for Amy if Amy would help out in the kitchen. Amy was relieved to hide out with Ly and Tu.

"Amy, did you bring homework?" asked Mom when things eventually slowed down.

Amy nodded as she rinsed a plate.

"Why don't you go work on it now," said Mom. She put a hand on Amy's shoulder. "You worked hard tonight."

"Thanks." Coming from Amy's mother, this was a big compliment.

Then Amy dried her hands and went out to the dining area. Fortunately Tyler and his family were long gone by now. In fact, there were only a few tables still full. Amy retrieved her backpack from one of the coat hooks by the door and went into the office to work on her homework. Her plan was to use the computer there to write and print out four copies of the play. But as she opened the main part of her backpack, she suddenly noticed what appeared to be another mysterious note in one of the partially zipped side pockets.

"Unreal!" she exclaimed as she unzipped the small pocket. Sure enough, it was another secret admirer note. This was unbelievable! Creepy even. And part of Amy wanted to wad the horrid thing up and throw it away, but another part of her was curious. And so she unfolded it and stared incredulously. The writing and pen color were exactly the same as the previous notes. But this time the message was a bit different.

Dear Amy,

I was really sorry to see you hurt like that. Please, don't take it personally. Sometimes we guys are just plain jerks. You are still the prettiest, smartest girl in the school. Don't be discouraged.

♥ YSA

Amy read the note again and again, trying to figure out who had written it and when it had been placed in her backpack. And why? What was the point? Surely this note wasn't really from Tyler. That was just too unbelievable. But then again, he had been here with his family tonight. Still, it was so weird. So weird, in fact, that it actually made her head hurt. Why would Tyler do something like this? Was it just a mean trick?

To be fair, Amy hadn't opened her backpack since Friday afternoon. So it seemed possible that someone besides Tyler might've slipped it in. Still, she wondered who would do this. Who would even care about how she'd been hurt? Well, besides her friends. Naturally, they cared.

Finally, Amy refolded the letter, stuffed it back into the pocket of her pack, and went to work on the play. Of course, now she was totally distracted. What if Tyler *had* put it there? And what if it had been his idea to come to the restaurant tonight just so he could do this? What if he really was sorry? Did she even care?

She focused her attention on writing the ending of their play on the computer. If she hurried, she might get it finished before closing. But as she wrote, she also made a few little minor changes. Nothing big, just improvements, really. Because, despite the fact that Amy didn't really care much about the play, she was still a perfectionist and she was still unable to turn in a project that wasn't top-notch.

"Time to go," called An. It was almost ten o'clock, and Amy was just printing out the last copy.

"Just a minute," said Amy as she stapled one of the scripts together.

"What's that?" asked An.

Amy explained. Then she also told An about receiving yet another secret admirer note.

"From that boy?" demanded An.

"I don't know," admitted Amy. "I mean, he was here, and my backpack was out there on a coat hook."

"That kid's got a lot of nerve." An laughed. "Or else he just has it really bad for you, Amy."

Amy gathered the last script, turned off the printer, and then stapled the script together. "You mean, if he's the one who wrote it. I could be wrong."

"Well, don't worry about it," said An as she turned off the light.

"You guys ready?" called Ly from the kitchen.

As the three of them drove home, Amy asked An if she would take her to see Miss McPhearson after church tomorrow.

"I can drop you off," said An. "But Ly will have to pick you up since I'm meeting someone for coffee. Do you mind, Ly?"

Amy could tell by the way her sister said *someone* that it was probably her boyfriend. She also knew that An didn't like to talk about him much. For one thing, he was not Vietnamese. For another thing, it usually made Ly jealous.

"As long as I get you before the lunch rush begins," said Ly.

"That's fine,"said Amy. "Even if I stay an hour, it won't be eleven yet."

"Okay. I think it's nice you don't mind visiting the Dragon Lady," said Ly.

"We don't call her that anymore," Amy pointed out.

"Maybe you don't, but Cara still does."

"I don't think Cara ever really understood Miss McPhearson," said Amy defensively. Cara had worked at the restaurant, as well as with Miss McPhearson, for a while. But she had eventually drifted to another town.

The next morning, after church, An dropped Amy at Miss McPhearson's house. Oddly enough it was one of those foggy days like the first time Amy had gone to see her. Only this time, Amy wasn't afraid. She'd called ahead of time, and the old woman was expecting her.

"Come in," Miss McPhearson said as she opened the door.

Amy handed her the pink heart-shaped box. "My friends and I made this for you," she told her. "We wanted to deliver it secretly, but I thought you might enjoy the company too."

"You thought right, Amy Ngo." Miss McPhearson smiled down at the box. "Very pretty. Thank you."

"You're welcome."

"And I have made us tea."

"You made it yourself?"

"Yes. I am on my own today. I've been giving Mrs. Platz Sundays off so she can go to church and whatnot."

"That's nice of you."

"I have everything all set for us in the library, Amy."

After they were seated, Miss McPhearson asked Amy to pour and serve the tea. Not a big surprise since she usually did this with Amy.

"I've missed you, Amy. You haven't been to see me in weeks." Miss McPearson's tone was deep and gruff, as usual, but Amy knew by now that there was kindness beneath it.

"I've missed you too," said Amy as she took a sip of tea.

"Tell me what you and your friends have been up to lately."

So Amy told her about making all the secret admirer valentines, although she didn't mention the Lonely Hearts Club part. "But you can't tell anyone," she said.

Miss McPhearson rolled her big owl eyes and said, "Humph. Who would I tell?"

"Well, we just wanted to keep the project top secret."

"Wherever do you girls come up with your ideas?"

Then Amy explained about how she'd gotten some mysterious notes. "That kind of inspired me to think of it."

"So, Amy Ngo, do you have a secret admirer?" Miss McPhearson's brows shot up. "Do tell."

Amy shrugged. "I guess I do. But I have to say, this secret admirer has made my life pretty miserable lately." Then she went ahead and told Miss McPhearson the rest of the story. She expected the old woman to laugh, but Miss McPhearson simply nodded with a look of sympathy and understanding.

"You and I are a bit alike, Amy Ngo," she said now.

"How is that?"

"We both have a fair amount of pride ... and I suppose that it can sometimes get in the way."

Amy nodded. "Yes. I think I sort of know what you mean."

"But I hope that you will learn to control it, Amy, instead of letting it control you."

Then Amy decided to tell Miss McPhearson about

how she'd asked God to help her—and how he had. "I realized that I had left God out of things … and that I need him to guide me."

"Then you are more wise than I was at your age," said Miss McPhearson.

"How is that?"

Miss McPhearson waved her hand in a dismissive way. "Old things, Amy, just water under the bridge now."

Now there was a quiet lull, and Amy decided to fill it. "Well, I did learn that it's totally stupid to be interested in boys—especially at my age."

Miss McPhearson nodded. "Yes … perhaps so … at least for now."

"Or maybe forever," proclaimed Amy. "Boys just end up hurting you."

Miss McPhearson sighed as she looked out the window that overlooked the ocean. It was still gray and foggy out there. "But here is a bit of advice from an old woman," she said quietly, then stopped.

"What is it?" asked Amy.

Miss McPhearson turned back to Amy now. "Do not allow yourself to become jaded, Amy Ngo."

"Jaded?" Amy frowned.

"Do not become bitter … welcome life, and it will welcome you."

Amy nodded now. She knew that Miss McPhearson

had not lived her life quite like this. Perhaps this was her way of saying she regretted it.

"It's like my father used to say," she continued. "But I'm afraid I didn't listen very well. I was too proud."

"What did he tell you?"

"Oh, it's an old adage ... about getting back on the horse that bucked you off. He had numerous ways of saying it. But his meaning was always clear."

"Oh ..."

"So, even if you think all boys are silly now ... someday you will need to reconsider." Miss McPhearson smiled. "But you are a smart girl, Amy Ngo. I'm sure you will figure things out."

chapter eleven

Amy tried to put thoughts of her secret admirer note completely out of her mind on Monday. She still thought there was a chance it might be Tyler. But at the same time she told herself that she simply did not care. Despite Miss McPhearson's encouragement, Amy still felt she was finished with caring about whether or not some stupid boy liked her. And her plan was to completely ignore the boy. Well, as much as she could anyway. She still had English to contend with, but fortunately their group project would be turned in today and that would be the end of it.

"Oh, Amy," said Chelsea when they met in front of the cafeteria before lunch. "I am so totally bummed!"

Amy looked at Chelsea and could see that something serious was wrong. "What is it?" Amy asked urgently. "Is it someone in your family? Is someone sick? Has there been a car wreck?"

"No." Chelsea was actually blinking back tears now. "Nothing like that."

"What is it then?" demanded Amy. "What happened?"

"Brett broke up with me."

Amy frowned. *Was that all?* "Oh ..."

"I know you don't care, Amy. You're probably glad he broke up. But I am totally devastated. I'm brokenhearted."

Amy knew that she should be kinder to her friend, but the truth was she really didn't care. The sooner Chelsea figured out that boys were stupid and mean and selfish, the better off everyone would be.

"I can't believe he did this to me," continued Chelsea. "And the day before the Valentine's Day dance too."

"So?" Amy just shrugged. "It's not that big of a deal."

"Maybe not to you ..." Now Chelsea really did start to cry, and Amy felt a little guilty for being so insensitive.

"I'm sorry," she told Chelsea. "I know it hurts when a boy you like doesn't like you back." Although, she wanted to add that she thought they both had invited these troubles — just by allowing themselves to be boy crazy. Still, she managed to keep those thoughts to herself. Maybe she could explain this to Chelsea later.

"I just can't believe he did it," continued Chelsea. "I mean, I went up to say hi and he just gave me the meanest look. And then he said he didn't like me anymore. Just like that."

"Well, Brett is stupid," said Amy.

"No, he's not."

Amy blinked. "Do you mean you still like him?"

"Of course!"

Amy rolled her eyes now. "Whatever."

"Will you talk to him for me, Amy?"

Now Amy laughed. "Sorry, Chelsea. But I am done with that kind of thing."

"Please, Amy." Chelsea looked desperate now. "I did it for you."

"And look where it got me. Look where it got you too."

Chelsea frowned.

"I'm sorry, Chelsea," said Amy in a gentler voice. "If I thought it was a good idea, I would talk to him. But, really, I'm so sick of the whole boy-crazy thing." Amy hadn't even told Chelsea about Tyler coming to the restaurant or her latest mystery note. Mostly Amy just wanted to forget the whole thing.

"Fine," said Chelsea.

"Come on," urged Amy. "Let's get lunch."

"But I might see him in there," said Chelsea.

"So?" Amy tugged on Chelsea's arm. "Just do like I do, Chelsea. Hold your head up and act like everything is fine."

Chelsea studied Amy for a moment then nodded. "Okay. I will."

Together the two of them marched into the cafeteria. And, walking right past the group of seventh grade boys, including both Tyler and Brett, they went and got into the lunch line. So there!

"See," said Amy. "That wasn't too bad, was it?"

"No ... it wasn't."

"And don't look back," warned Amy.

They got their food, and Amy was relieved to join their other friends. Chelsea told them about her recent heartbreak.

"See," said Carlie. "That's what happens."

"You don't have to be happy about it," said Chelsea.

"I think everyone gets their heart broken at some time in her life," said Emily. "I've read enough poetry to believe this is true."

"But you shouldn't go out there looking for it," said Morgan.

"Probably not," said Emily. "But I'm sure it will happen to all of us eventually."

"It sounds horrible," said Carlie.

"It is," admitted Chelsea.

Then Amy told them about what Miss McPhearson had said to her yesterday. "I think she had her heart broken too," she said finally.

"I knew it," said Emily. "Remember I thought she'd had some romantic tragedy."

"But you know what she said," continued Amy.

"What?" they all asked.

"She said that you shouldn't become bitter. She said not to allow pride to keep you from trying again ... or something like that."

"Well, maybe when you're older," said Morgan.

"Like eighteen," added Carlie. "My dad doesn't want me to have a boyfriend until I'm eighteen."

They laughed.

"I'm guessing your dad is in for a big surprise," said Chelsea.

"Maybe sixteen," said Carlie.

"I don't want a boyfriend until God tells me I'm old enough," proclaimed Morgan.

"Me too," said Emily.

"Ditto," added Amy.

"I'm with you guys," said Carlie.

"I don't know ..." Chelsea frowned. "Do you think God will actually do that? I mean, what's he going to do — write it in the sky?"

"He has his ways," said Morgan.

Then the bell rang, and it was time to head for class. As the afternoon wore on, Amy began to dread the idea of English class. She didn't want to sit in the small group with Tyler again. It was actually making her stomach hurt, and she wondered if she wasn't getting an ulcer. It wouldn't have been that bad if she hadn't gotten that last note — the one at the restaurant. Still, as she went to English she reminded herself of what she'd said to Chelsea. Hold your head high and just act perfectly normal.

"Here are the copies of the play," she told her group as

soon as they sat down. "Maybe we should just read them to ourselves."

"But Mrs. Hilliard said we're supposed to practice," said Myrna.

Amy glanced at the clock. "Well, let's skim them and then we can practice. Okay?"

At least this bought Amy enough time to calm down. Because the first thing she'd noticed was that Tyler was still using the pen that was the same color as the one that had written her mystery notes. She wished she could get another peek at his handwriting. But, at the same time, she didn't want to think about it. She just wanted to move on.

Finally they had skimmed the play, read their parts, and Amy turned in their project just before the bell rang. It was all she could do to control herself from cheering. The project was over. Well, other than the competition part tomorrow. But Amy felt fairly certain that their play, which in her opinion wasn't very good, could not possibly win.

"Time to go make decorations," announced Morgan as the girls gathered in the locker bay.

"I don't even want to now," complained Chelsea. She still looked pretty bummed, and her eyes were puffy from crying.

"This was your idea in the first place," pointed out Carlie.

"And Amy's too," added Chelsea in a sharp tone.

"No, it wasn't," protested Amy.

Naturally, this resulted in a big argument about who had wanted to go to the dance, who had been boy crazy, and who wanted to be in Honor Society. And, of course, no one could remember it quite right. And, sure, maybe Amy had originally wanted to go to the dance, but that had all changed. Now, as they headed to the room where they were supposed to help with decorations, she couldn't care less about some stupid dance, and the last thing she wanted was to actually go out on the dance floor and dance.

"Hey, there's Second Chair and her friends," said Oliver Fitzgerald when the girls went to the classroom that was filled with what were obviously the materials for decorations. It was like a sea of red, pink, and white paper and balloons.

"You're here," said Vanessa Price. "Great." Then she immediately assigned them to the boring task of cutting out what seemed like hundreds of various-sized paper hearts. "Any questions?" she said.

"Do we really have to do this?" asked Carlie.

Vanessa smiled in a slightly smug way. "No one is making you. But someday you will be thankful that you did. We all did it at one time."

"We're fine,"Emily assured her as she picked up a pair of scissors.

"Good." Vanessa nodded. "Then I'll leave you to

it. And when you're done, just stack everything in that office."

"How about the balloons?" asked Oliver.

"Fill those garbage bags and then put them on the stage until tomorrow. We'll start decorating the cafeteria after lunch." She grinned. "We get the whole afternoon off. And then you guys will take over for us right after seventh. That gives us time to clean up."

"How do we know what to do?" asked Chelsea.

"Oliver will still be there to supervise. The dance starts at three thirty, so you'll have to work fast."

"And then we can go home?" asked Amy hopefully.

Vanessa frowned. "No, of course not. You'll also be doing the teardown afterward. *And* we do expect you to attend the dance — any future Honor Society members must be there."

Chelsea let out a groan.

"Attitude check," said Vanessa brightly. Then she waved good-bye and left the room.

"You girls are really paying your dues," said Oliver as they settled into cutting out hearts.

"What about you?" asked Amy suddenly. "Why are you here?"

Oliver grinned sheepishly. "I guess I'm paying my dues too."

"Why?" asked Emily. "I thought you were an eighth grader."

"I missed the planning meeting." He chuckled. "And so I was appointed head balloon blower."

"Lucky you," said Morgan.

"Oh, that's okay," said Amy quickly. "Oliver is just full of hot air."

They all laughed. And for the next few hours they continued to tease and joke and really, it wasn't too terrible. Although Amy's hands were seriously tired by the time they stacked the hearts in the office.

"Oliver's kind of nice," said Morgan as they walked home.

"Yeah," said Emily. "You always make him sound so terrible, Amy. He's actually pretty funny."

"You mean *funny* looking," joked Amy. And when her friends laughed, she felt bad and almost told them about how Oliver had actually come to her defense that day when Tyler had publicly humiliated her. But she didn't. Most of all she just wanted to forget that it had ever happened.

chapter twelve

"You girls sure made a lot of folks happy this morning," said Morgan's grandmother as she pulled up at the school. They'd just finished delivering the last of their Lonely Hearts Club valentines, and Amy had been worried that they would be late, but now it looked like they were just fine.

"And this one is for you, Mrs. Evans," said Amy as she handed the last heart to her from the backseat.

"Why, thank you very much," said Morgan's grandma. "And you girls tell all your friends thank you for me, won't you?"

"You're not supposed to know that it's from us," pointed out Morgan as she got her backpack.

"Oh, that's right." Her grandma nodded and placed a finger to her lips. "I'll pretend that I found it on my doorstep."

"Just like the one we left at Mom's shop," said Morgan.

"And for Mr. Greeley and the others," said Amy happily. It had been such fun to sneak up to houses and plant their surprises in front of the doors. They had considered ringing doorbells, but worried they might wake someone up.

"Have a good day, girls!" called Grandma.

Amy and Morgan thanked her and waved, then walked up to the school. Amy noticed that a lot of the other girls were kind of dressed up. Probably in anticipation of the "big" Valentine's Day dance that would be right after school. And, to be honest, at this same time last week, Amy thought that she'd have been dressed up too. But considering how things had gone, Amy had no big expectations for the dance. And besides jeans and a pink sweater, which really weren't very festive, Amy looked pretty much like normal.

Thoughts of the dance were just an irritation now. Mostly she just wanted to get the decorating done, the dance over with, the decorations stripped down, and then she would be perfectly happy to go work at the restaurant tonight. An said there were lots of reservations. And the plan was to put a red rose and a candle on each table. That was An's idea and something new for them. Still, it would be fun. More fun than this stupid old dance!

"We got them all sent," said Emily when Amy and Morgan found her and Carlie.

"Did anyone see you?" asked Amy.

"I don't think so," said Emily.

"We took turns watching for each other," explained Carlie.

"How did your deliveries go?" asked Emily.

"Great," said Morgan.

"Hey, there's Chelsea," said Carlie.

Amy was slightly surprised to see that even Chelsea hadn't dressed up for Valentine's Day. But then Chelsea had just had her heart broken — why would she want to dress up?

"How did the deliveries go?" asked Amy.

"Pretty good," said Chelsea. Then she smiled. "Except that Mrs. Drimmel sort of caught me."

"Sort of?" Emily frowned. Amy knew that Mrs. Drimmel was Emily's special friend. It had been her idea to give the librarian a valentine.

"Well, I just played dumb," said Chelsea. "I said someone had handed this to me and asked me to deliver it to the library. I pretended not to even know who she was. I think it worked."

"Oh, good!" Emily sighed in relief.

They all shared various interesting stories, and soon it was time to get to class. Amy hurried to band, but then wondered if Oliver had possibly gotten his valentine yet. Surely he would never guess that she'd had anything to do with it. At least she hoped not. She also hoped that he wouldn't have it with him in band. But, just in case, she prepared herself to act innocent and nonchalant.

"Hey, Second Chair," he said as she went in and hung up her coat.

"Hey, Hot Air," she shot back at him, pleased with her quick comeback.

He laughed. "That's a good one."

"Do you have any hot air left after yesterday?" she asked.

"I have enough to keep my chair," he said as he picked up his clarinet and played a perfect stanza without even warming up.

She frowned. "You're really going to make this hard on me, aren't you?"

"You'll get your chance, Second Chair." He laughed. "When I go to high school, that is."

She scowled at him and shook her fist. But, to her surprise, she no longer felt angry. And that felt good!

Throughout the day, Amy noticed that a number of kids had exchanged valentines — and she felt sort of badly that she hadn't thought to send her very best friends valentines. But they'd been so busy making ones for the Lonely Hearts Club that it hadn't even occurred to her. She laughed to think of this now. Maybe they should've included themselves on that list since they were, in a way, lonely hearts too. No, she decided they were not. They had each other! But as Amy continued through her day, she was also pleased to see some of the less-popular kids — the loners — carrying around the valentines that she and her friends had made. That made her feel good inside.

"This is so cool," said Emily as they sat together for lunch.

"I know," gushed Amy. "I saw Myrna Shaft, the girl in my English class, clutching her valentine like it was made of gold or contained chocolate."

"And you won't believe it," said Morgan, "but I actually witnessed Derrick opening his this morning."

"No way!" shrieked Emily. "Tell us! What happened?"

"Well, I was trying to be really discrete. I was squatting down by my locker, trying to find something buried down on the bottom. Then I noticed what he was doing, so I just stayed there and pretended to be looking at something inside my notebook, but the whole time I was watching him. He got this suspicious look as he opened the envelope and he read it really quickly, and then he glanced all around like he was trying to see who sent it. Then he looked at the card again and he just kept staring at it. Seriously, it was like he stared at it for several minutes. My knees were actually getting stiff. Then he kind of smiled and just slipped it into his backpack and walked away. It seemed like he actually had a little spring in his step too. I can't believe I'm saying this, but it was really sort of sweet."

"That's awesome," said Amy.

Chelsea nodded. "That's so cool that you thought to send it to him, Emily."

"Well, you guys know how his home life is pretty harsh," said Emily.

"Yeah," said Carlie. "He probably really needed something like that."

Amy patted Emily on the back. "Good for you for remembering him."

They shared a few more good lonely hearts stories and then it was time to go to class. Amy felt happy as she went to Algebra Two. And even though Tyler was in that class, she told herself that it didn't matter. Of course, when it was time for English she wasn't too sure. But at least they didn't have to sit in their small groups.

Of course, as it turned out, their play won first prize! Go figure. Now, normally there was nothing that pleased Amy more than being first, best, or smartest in the class. But not today.

"And now," said Mrs. Hilliard, "If our winners will please come up and read their play." She began clapping, and the rest of the class obediently followed.

Still, it wasn't as bad as Amy expected as she and Tyler and Myrna and Bruce read their play. And to her surprise, it seemed the class liked it too. Their prizes for winning first place were heart-shaped boxes of chocolates. Amy planned to share hers with her friends while they decorated for the dance.

"Good job on the play," Tyler said as Amy was just heading for the door.

She was stunned that he had actually spoken to her. She just blinked then said, "Thanks, you too." Then she took off. Hopefully that would be the last conversation they would ever share. Now Amy hurried to the cafeteria. When she got there, Oliver seemed a little distraught.

"What's wrong?" she asked.

He waved his hand to piles of hearts, crepe paper, balloons ... all over the place. "They didn't do hardly anything," he told her. "The committee just sort of played around, and now we have thirty minutes to get this all up."

"Tell us what to do," said Morgan, who had come in right behind Amy. Soon all five girls were working, scurrying around climbing ladders and taping up hearts and hearts and more hearts — stringing crepe paper and balloons haphazardly about. Talk about a decorating frenzy!

"Hey, this doesn't look half bad," said Morgan as she stepped back to survey their work.

"We have four more minutes," yelled Amy. "Keep working!"

The DJ in charge of music laughed from up in front where he was sitting with his machines. "You girls are fun to watch," he called out as he put on a song with an upbeat tempo. Thanks to the music, they seemed to actually work faster.

"Time!" yelled Oliver. Just then he dumped what was left of a bag of balloons, spilling a pool of red, pink, and white across the floor. "This is as good as it gets, girls."

"Whew!" said Emily, actually wiping sweat from her brow.

"Now, can we get out of here?" begged Carlie.

"Not if you're serious about Honor Society," said Oliver. "Vanessa was not kidding yesterday."

"Can we at least have a bathroom break?" demanded Morgan.

Oliver grinned. "Yeah. But don't forget to come back."

As the five of them left, feeling frazzled and messy, they saw kids starting to trickle in. And, naturally, everyone else looked clean and stylish and ready for the big event.

"Did you bring anything to change into for the dance?" Amy asked Chelsea as they went into the girls' restroom.

"Are you kidding?" Chelsea frowned into the mirror above the sink as she washed her hands. "What would be the point?"

"And what's the point of going back in there?" asked Carlie. "All we'll do is stand around like a bunch of misfits."

"We're going back there because we said we would," said Emily as she attempted to scrub red crepe paper stains from her fingers.

"At least they have refreshments," said Morgan. "I'm hungry."

"That's right," said Carlie. "We better get back there before they're all gone."

So they finished cleaning up and went back and got refreshments. Then they stood along the sidelines and watched as kids, mostly the eighth graders, started to dance.

"They look so silly," said Emily as she took a bite of a heart-shaped cookie.

"Some of those boys could use dancing lessons," added Morgan.

"You'll never catch me out there," said Carlie.

Amy nodded like she agreed, but the truth was, a tiny part of her still wanted to be out there. Okay, it was a very teeny tiny part. But she couldn't deny that it was there. And maybe that's what Miss McPhearson had been talking about the other day, that willingness to get back on a horse that had dumped you. Still, Amy knew it wouldn't be today. Today would be way too soon. And that was just fine.

The girls continued to cluster together, talking and joking like it was no big deal. But all of them wished that this dance would end so they could tear down the decorations and go home. And then, more than midway through the dance, a surprising thing happened. Well, at least it shocked Amy. She couldn't tell if her friends were surprised or not.

It started when Jeff Sanders and Enrico Valdez came over to their group. The guys kind of joked around a little and finally Jeff asked Emily to dance with him and then Enrico asked Carlie. Well, it was plain that both girls were embarrassed and didn't know what to do. Especially Carlie! Her cheeks turned bright pink. But Amy and Chelsea and Morgan all encouraged them to go out there and dance.

"Have fun," said Chelsea.

"Show them how it's done," Morgan teased.

"Go for it," said Amy. The truth was she was actually feeling a little sorry for the guys. Jeff and Enrico looked totally uncomfortable, like they wished they hadn't taken such a risk. But soon the two couples were out there dancing with the others.

And then the strangest thing imaginable happened. At least Amy thought so. She had no idea what Morgan thought just then. But Amy could've fallen over from shock when Derrick Smith came over to their group. All three remaining girls looked totally stunned to see him. But Derrick went directly to Morgan. He smiled shyly and asked, "So, Morgan, do ya'wanna dance?"

Morgan turned and looked at Amy and Chelsea with wide eyes, like she didn't know what to do.

"Go for it," said Amy for the second time. She was trying not to giggle at the absurdity of their one-time enemy actually asking one of them to dance. Who would've guessed?

Then Morgan actually grinned as she poked Derrick in the arm and said, "Hey, why not?" And then she went out to the dance floor and, once out there, she even did her Electric Porcupine dance. And then all three of their friends went on to dance to the next song as well. It was only Chelsea and Amy watching from the sidelines now. But Amy was thankful that at least she wasn't standing there alone.

"Looks like we're the wallflowers today," said Chelsea in a glum tone.

"Welcome to the Lonely Hearts Club." Amy kind of laughed.

"Maybe we should get ourselves membership pins," said Chelsea.

"Or maybe not ..." said Amy as she noticed that Brett Woods seemed to be slowly coming their way. But Chelsea had her back to him and no idea what was about to happen. Brett tapped Chelsea on the shoulder, and the next thing Amy knew, those two were out on the dance floor.

Okay, suddenly this wasn't so funny, and it sure wasn't fun. Amy was all alone. Queen of the Lonely Hearts Club. A wallflower that no one wanted to pick. She was about to turn and make a quick exit when she saw, of all people, Tyler Epperson walking straight toward her! But at the same time she saw Oliver coming from the other direction. She figured Oliver was probably going to remind her that they had to stay for teardown. And she had no idea what Tyler wanted, but her heart pounded madly as both boys stood before her.

Oliver glanced at Tyler. "So, are you going to ask Amy to dance?" he asked. And Amy felt her cheeks getting flushed. This was way too embarrassing.

"Yeah, I guess so ..." Tyler nodded nervously.

"Well, so was I," announced Oliver. Now he turned to Amy. "So, there you have it, Second Chair — two guys asking you to dance. Who do you choose?"

Amy looked at Tyler now, remembering her crush and then how she'd been crushed. Next she looked at Oliver, remembering all the teasing — and then how he'd stood up and defended her against Tyler.

"I will dance with you, Oliver," she proclaimed.

He grinned.

"Maybe some other time," she said casually to Tyler. Then she walked onto the dance floor with a guy she had previously categorized as the "geekiest" boy in school. But now she realized that she had been wrong. Oliver was actually okay. And she even danced two dances with him. And, as it turned out, they were the last two dances.

"Thanks," he told her when the second dance ended. "You're a good sport, Second Chair."

She smiled. "Thank you."

"And, just so you know ..." He winked at her as he jerked his thumb to his chest. "Y.S.A."

She blinked in surprise. "You?"

"Now you girls have fun tearing this all down." And then he took off and didn't even stick around to help.

Soon the cafeteria was emptied — except for the five girls and all the valentine decorations.

"Hey, where did Oliver go?" demanded Morgan. "I thought he was supposed to help tear down."

"He, uh, I think he had to leave," said Amy quickly. "Besides we should have this done in no time." Then she grabbed a plastic fork from the picked-clean refreshment table and stabbed a balloon, resulting in a loud POP. "See, it's easy." She giggled, and before long they were all stabbing balloons. And then they were ripping down crepe paper and tearing into the hearts, stuffing them into the big black trash bags. And before long, the whole cafeteria was back to normal.

"Too bad the refreshments are all gone," said Carlie. "I'm hungry now."

"Hey," said Amy as she picked up her backpack. "I have a valentine to share with you guys." So she flopped down on the floor, and her friends sat around her, waiting as she opened up the heart-shaped box of chocolates and passed it around.

"The dance was fun," said Emily as she took a bite of a chocolate.

"Yeah," said Morgan. "Can you guys believe I actually danced with Derrick Smith?"

They all laughed.

"I was so glad you didn't say no to him," admitted

Amy. "Especially after you told us about how he acted when he got his valentine."

"Yeah. That would've been pretty harsh," said Morgan.

"And *you* dancing with Oliver?" said Chelsea. "What was up with that, Amy?"

"Oliver is a good guy." No way was Amy going to tell them, or anyone else for that matter, what Oliver had confessed to her on the dance floor. That would be her secret.

"Yeah, so maybe all guys aren't dogs after all," said Carlie quietly.

"Even so," said Amy as she held up the heart-shaped lid of the chocolate box in one hand and a chocolate in the other. "I hereby vow that only God — *not a guy* — is going to rule *my* heart!"

"Here-here!" echoed Morgan. She held up a chocolate too.

And so they all took another chocolate, holding them up like Amy was doing — sort of like making a toast — and they all repeated the exact same thing that Amy had just said.

"Only God rules our hearts!" said Amy happily.

"Rainbow Rules!" yelled Morgan. They all echoed her. And Amy knew that what she and her friends shared — a love for God and a love for each other — would take them through whatever lay ahead.

Girls of Harbor View by Melody Carlson!

Harbor view was no place for a girl ... until now. Meet Morgan, Amy, Carlie, and Emily, unlikely friends brought together when they come to live in the Harbor View Trailer Park. Discover what happens when they join forces to make their world a better place.

Girl Power

Softcover: 978-0-310-73045-3

Take Charge

Softcover: 978-0-310-73046-0

Raising Faith

Softcover: 978-0-310-73047-7

Secret Admirer

Softcover: 978-0-310-73048-4

Available in stores and online!

Visit www.zondervan.com/teen